IN UNHALLOWED REST

A Sherlock Holmes Adventure

John Sutton

Paperback ISBN 978-1-78705-177-5
ePub ISBN 978-1-78705-178-2
PDF ISBN 978-1-78705-179-9

Published in the UK by MX Publishing
335 Princess Park Manor, Royal Drive,
London, N11 3GX
www.mxpublishing.co.uk

Cover design by Brian Belanger

Chapter One

A scrap of paper is, by definition, worthless since, by its description, it contains little of any interest; while a piece of paper may contain information of some import. I shall, therefore, refer to the item that had been pushed through my letter box as a piece. Upon opening the folded paper, I saw that it contained all but the briefest of messages, requesting both Holmes and I to meet with the unknown writer at four o'clock the same day, under the large clock in Waterloo railway station. I was also informed that the proposed meeting was a matter of life and death to the writer. That was all.

Having spent most of the morning discussing the dispositions of a distant relative's considerably large estate and learning that my name did not appear in even a small beneficent portion within her proposed Will, I returned somewhat deflated to our rooms in Baker street. Mrs. Hudson had previously informed me that she would be away for most of the day, visiting her sister and I knew that Holmes was in Godalming and would not be back until later that evening, thus the day, or what remained of it, was left at my disposal.

My fascination with mysteries is well documented so it will be of little surprise to the reader to learn that I decided to do as I had been most mysteriously requested.

At precisely five minutes to four that afternoon, I stood under the famous time piece and awaited the outcome of my journey from my lodgings. As I am committed to the belief that staring is a most unseemly practice I therefore contented myself with an occasional glance at the numerous railway platforms, which allowed me a peripheral visual comprehension of my present surroundings. From my position I noticed the general comings and goings of a busy railway station, but little attracted my attention.

It was, therefore, something of a small shock to my system as I felt an urgent tug on the right-hand cuff of my overcoat. Turning about, I suffered another shock that took all my self-control in order not to shrink back. The face before me evidenced such a degree of suffering that it bore little resemblance to a living soul. The eyes peered furtively from within two dark pits, and the pallor of the entire countenance was that of a corpse. When the voice spoke, it was hoarse and bore a distinct tremor in its utterance.

"Mr. Holmes? croaked the voice.
"No, I am not he. My name is Watson," I managed to reply. "Who might I have the pleasure of addressing?"

The corpse grabbed my right hand and wrung the same with such intensity that I feared he might dislocate my wrist.

"Thank God you have come" he whispered. Then, in a more controlled voice he spoke again. "Please forgive me. My name is Simon Brinton". "My dear Brinton, do compose yourself" said I, for it appeared to me that the man was nearing the stages of imminent collapse.

At my words the other seemed to assume a greater degree of control than he had previously evidenced. "I am sorry

Dr. Watson" he said. "I have had little rest for the past few days; such has been my anxiety upon a matter". "Come come Brinton" I said. "Nothing surely maybe so distressful as to place you within the condition you now evidence most plainly".

The other attempted the beginnings of what I took to be a rueful smile - then gave up entirely.

"Would not the proximity of the most horrendous and terrible death cause you some distress Dr. Watson?" Brinton murmured.

"But are you ill my dear fellow?" I enquired. "I must say that your physical appearance might suggest the same might be true". "Ill, no; near death most decidedly my dear doctor" cackled the other, cautiously peering about himself in the most concerning fashion. "I am without assistance or comfort of any nature, and I fear I have but few hours remaining before I shall enter a hell far more terrible than any described in the good book".

I would normally have terminated the situation then and there and moved away as fast as possible from the man, but something about his demeanour made me stay. I perceived that Brinton's condition was not the result of insanity but of a dreadful fear for his very life. This both interested and fascinated my inquisitive nature. "My dear Brinton, please calm yourself. I see that you are quite beset with fright. Let me suggest we take a carriage to my club where, are suitable refreshment, you may advise me of the cause of your present discomfort. Perhaps I may be able to allay your obvious fears". At my words Brinton again grabbed my right hand. "Oh, Dr. Watson, if only that might be possible" he groaned weakly. "But I fear that whatever actions you may consider will already be too late to avert my imminent doom". With that Brinton's face regained the look of abject terror that had been so apparent on our meeting.

"Tut tut" I said. "Things are never as bad as you believe them to be. Now, let us obtain the services of a cabbie and shortly you may acquaint me with the circumstances that have given rise to your condition". Taking Brinton's arm, I guided the poor fellow to a waiting cab and instructed the driver to take us to a small private hotel, just off Bedford Square where, we would be able to talk in some privacy. We spoke little during the short journey to our destination and, in fact, it was not until after Brinton had consumed his second balloon of Napoleon within the confines of a large winged leather chair, that I spoke to him further on the current matter – the subject of his present state. "Now" said I, "perhaps you may feel able to tell me of what you are so terribly afraid". "I feel you will not believe me Dr. Watson" replied Brinton. "Let me be the judge of that my friend" said I: please begin". Taking another large swallow of his brandy, Brinton leant forward in his chair and began his story.

'I am a solicitor and a partner in a medium sized practice in Colchester, a medium sized town situated in the north-east of Essex,' he began. ' I served my Articles of Clerkship with a local firm of solicitors, Messrs. Martell & Button and, upon qualifying as a solicitor of the Supreme Court, offered a position in the firm. Within the space of a further year, I was further offered a junior partnership therein. During this period, I had purchased a small, yet comfortable house in the more sought-after section of the town and settled down to enjoy the social benefits and financial rewards of a successful young lawyer.

A year after my admission to the partnership, Martell & Button had been consulted late one winter's afternoon, by a certain Sir Eldon Manning seeking to acquire a substantial property, known as Bascott Hall, in the neighbouring county of Suffolk. Sir Eldon, it appeared, was lately retired as Her Majesty's Ambassador to Transylvania and, wishing to retire from the hustle and bustle of the Foreign Office, had discovered the presence of the land and property in question.

Both Martell and Button were of an age and disposition where travel, even for the shortest distance, might be avoided if possible; and they kindly offered me the opportunity to introduce myself to the new client with the advices that an involvement with such an eminently august personage as Sir Eldon could not but elevate my own personal standing within the local community. I virtually jumped at the chance, and an evening meeting at a local hotel had been arranged where Sir Eldon had taken temporary lodgings until the transaction to acquire Bascott Hall had been completed.

Upon our initial meeting, I was somewhat surprised at the appearance of my potential client. Sir Eldon must have been in his late fifties or early sixties. Yet the man who welcomed me into the hotel and offered me refreshment seemed hardly into his late thirties. Eldon was above medium height, yet slight of build. Though affable, and most courteous beyond question, there was something about the man that caused within me a most definite sense of unease. However, any misgivings that I may have sensed at that time, were soon forgotten we both began discussion on the details of the imminent purchase of Bascott Hall. Sir Eldon had excused the time of the meeting with the comment that he rarely rose before noon each day and, wishing to avoid the hurly burly of the hotel's guests, remained in his suite of rooms until some semblance of peace and quiet descended on the hotel. This excuse appeared quite plausible and acceptable to my mind.

Upon the completion of our discussions, Sir Eldon had insisted that I, as his obviously selected solicitor, join him for dinner. I was about to reply that my own housekeeper would have set food waiting at my own home, but any thought of even suggesting this fact disappeared upon the appearance of the most beautiful girl that I had ever seen in my life. Sir Eldon, noticing the effect of the girl's arrival upon me, quickly introduced the young lady as his daughter, Magda.

I must confess that I am unable to recall exact details of the remainder of the first evening that I met Magda. The deep violet eyes that sought and held my own were of such depth and luminosity, and the soft deep petals of those divine lips from which came forth words of such gentle content, beguiled me so that, by the arrival of the second course of the meal, I confess that I had fallen completely in love with the beautiful creature. It will suffice that, by the time I finally made my farewells that night, I had both sought and obtained Sir Eldon's permission to call upon Magda.

During the weeks that followed the completion of the purchase of Bascott Hall, I became a regular visitor to the property. Magda appeared to return the same intensity of passion for me as I had for her, and her father seemed more than satisfied upon the situation that existed.

The fact that Sir Eldon was never present during my daytime visits has been easily explained away by the fact that, as a retired gentleman, rose and ate late and, therefore, did not wish to receive visitors until the evening hours. This fact bothered me little since it allowed me unlimited hours with my new love without interruption.

A scant six months after our initial meeting, I asked Sir Eldon for his daughter's hand, and was delighted when the Baronet happily informed me that nothing would give him greater pleasure than to welcome me into his family. The banns were called at the local church in the small hamlet of Dedham, the closest village to Bascott Hall and shortly afterwards, Magda and I were married.

Sir Eldon had insisted on giving us a house as a wedding gift and Grafton Grange, forming a part of Sir Eldon's estate, was completely redecorated and furnished to our, or more correctly Magda's exact wishes for this purpose. Having little use for the same, I sold my small property in Colchester at quite a profit and, shortly after Christmas of that year, my wife and I settled comfortably into our new home. I purchased a gig which allowed me to travel the few miles from the Grange to Colchester within the hour. Martell and Button, overjoyed at the prospect of the possible future business that would accumulate from a junior partner, now so well connected, immediately increased my partnership salary. Thus, that precise moment in time, I could not have been more satisfied with my life.

Each morning, after I shaved and breakfasted, I would leave for my busy practice in Colchester, while Magda organised the staff in the daily matters of house management. Each evening, I would return to the loving arms of my darling wife, and the peace and tranquillity of a secluded country mansion. As is sometimes the way with newlyweds, we tended to cultivate few new friends, preferring to spend such free time as there was by ourselves. The only exception to this lifestyle was our requested attendance at the lavish parties held by Sir Eldon upon the first Saturday of each month. For my own part, I was little concerned whether we attended these soirées or not but, in order to please Magda, I accepted, the monthly meetings as part of my family duty.

By the standards of the age, the parties were quite wild affairs. Normally white tie but, on occasions in costume, they would last until nearly dawn. Those guests who had not been invited for the weekend always departing a few hours before sunrise. Sir Eldon's retirement from public life had not diminished his youthful zest for rarely were any of the guests over the age of thirty. This fact alone might have caused another to ponder on Sir Eldon's circle of acquaintances – where were the older people? However, I was far too occupied in attending upon my lovely wife and the thought never crossed my mind.

In the April of the year following our marriage, Magda celebrated her eighteenth birthday. Sir Eldon informed me that the eighteenth birthday was considered a momentous event in the area of Transylvania where Magda had been born, and proposed to hold a celebration at Bascott Hall – to which many of his eastern European friends would be

8

invited. I was somewhat concerned when Sir Eldon informed that, on the night in question, Magda would be obliged to remain at the Hall without her husband. Sir Eldon explained the reason for this somewhat odd insistence was a local Transylvanian custom celebrating a young girl's entry into womanhood, at which only Transylvanians might be present.

On the day prior to the party the local doctor confirmed that Magda was with child. You may imagine that I was ecstatic upon receiving the news and could hardly wait to break the same to her father. However, I bided my time until we arrived at the Hall the following night.

On our arrival at Bascott Hall, I noticed that Magda had evidenced a degree of nervousness - both on our journey to the Hall and, more so, upon our entrance into the large reception room. My attempts to comfort and assure my wife that, rather than being nervous, she should be delighted at the opportunity to celebrate her birthday and, more to the point, announce their forthcoming happy and joyous event, seemed to have little result.

Being upon nodding acquaintance with most of the assembled guests and, having made my customary salutations to those others upon our arrival, I made my way to Sir Eldon, greeted him warmly and informed him upon our forthcoming event. At the impart of my news, Sir Eldon could not have appeared more delighted. Kissing his daughter and shaking my hand far more than was required, he joyously announced to the other guests his impending advancement to grandfather following which, a ripple of congratulatory applause ran through the room. I noticed that there appeared to be some ten Transylvanians attending the party. Grouped to the right of Sir Eldon, they stood out starkly amongst the rest of the guests. They were dressed in black, men and ladies. Their apparel contrasted strongly with the sallow complexions that each bore upon their unsmiling faces. Their collective presence causing a dark blot on the multitudinous hues that caparisoned brightly among the other ladies of the party. As the other guests appeared to take little notice of the eastern European section of the assembled throng, I decided to do likewise.

The evening passed quite quickly and it, therefore, came as some surprise to me when Sir Eldon announced that the official evening's entertainment was nearing its close. As agreed with Sir Eldon, I took sad leave of my wife, Sir Eldon and such of those guests who had not already departed, and made my way back to The Grange, content that whatever ceremony Magda was to fulfil, she would be perfectly safe in the company of her adoring father.

The following morning a servant arrived at the Grange, bearing a brief message from Sir Eldon. It appeared that the festivities of the previous evening had been a little too much for Magda and she would rest at Bascott Hall for the remainder of the day, but would be home without fail by dusk. Promptly at nightfall Magda arrived back at The Grange. Sign of any former disposition under which she allegedly endured appeared to have left her, for she was as bright and gay as the day on which I had married her.

Upon my questions to her as to the nature of the secret ceremony, Magda was able to reply that the entire thing had been a most awful bore and that she would not trouble me in its description. Most joyous at the safe return of my beloved wife for, in fact, though we had been parted for only a matter of hours, I had missed her sorely, I desisted in my questions and following a simple supper, we both retired to bed.

The following weeks were filled with preparations for the coming birth for, although the actual event was several months away, Sir Eldon insisted on turning the large second bedroom into the new nursery and, further, would not countenance any but he to pay for the works involved.

At this point in the narrative, I interrupted Brinton to offer him another glass of brandy, which he readily accepted. Brinton then continued.

About six weeks ago, Magda began to evidence signs of excessive tiredness. Although I was away at my office, I would learn upon my arrival home that my wife, upon occasions, had remained in her bed for most of the day. I consulted the local doctor and was informed that this weariness was often a by-product of pregnancy and thus satisfied myself that there was no undue need for concern. However, a short while later, a most alarming event occurred.

As an individual I had always enjoyed a good night's sleep. Problems that might have besought we throughout the day normally disappeared immediately on the soft embrace of a long, soundless and uninterrupted sleep. It came as somewhat of a surprise, therefore, having awakened one night from a reason that I was unable to identify, I discovered that my wife was not in the bed that we shared. Not unduly perturbed, I lit a bedside candle but was unable to discover her whereabouts within the confines of the large bedroom. A hurried search of the entire house resulted in nothing and justifiably more than concerned, now more than concerned at her absence, I lit a lantern and made his way into the considerable grounds that encompassed the building. A half hour's search produced scant evidence of my missing wife and I was about to return to the house when I heard the rustle of a heavy body's passage in the undergrowth of the small wood that abutted the property. Making my way in the direction of the sound, I beheld a most alarming vision. Magda, for it was she, stood before my astonished eyes. Yet the person that stood before me in the dim light of the lantern's flickering flame, bore little resemblance to the lovely creature I had so recently wed. The vision stared with eyes that saw nothing. The expensive nightdress was crumpled in the most severe fashion and bore dark stains that ran from throat to hem. I instinctively called out her name, but the vision seemed not to hear my voice. Moving towards my wife, I touched her arm. She turned almost savagely on me and uttered a sound that was more a snarl than a grunt. For a moment her eyes focussed, and they were the eyes of an enraged beast. Her reaction caused me to shudder involuntarily and draw away from the form that I so adored. There was something terribly wrong with her mouth but, in my shocked senses, I was unable to determine exactly what. Suddenly Magda uttered a dreadful groan and fell senseless to the ground.

Horrified at my wife's condition, I lifted the senseless form and carried her into the house. The doctor was summoned and, after an extensive examination of my wife, declared that he could find little trace of any serious ailment and advised me that he believed his wife's condition was brought on by her pregnancy, prescribing rest and a change of diet.

Following the doctor's advice, Magda's health appeared to improve and, over the next few weeks, she returned to the vitality and vigour of her former self. If any change might be noticed in my wife, it was her preference for shade against the bright sunlight of day. Magda rested during most of the hours of daylight, rising only after the twilight and darkness of night. Initially, I paid scant attention to this fact. The doctor had prescribed extensive rest and that was what Magda wishes.

However, some weeks later an event occurred which resulted in my attempt to contact either you or Mister Holmes. In order to permit my wife as much undisturbed sleep as was possible, I had taken to sleeping in one of the guest rooms. On the night in question, I experienced what, in my own words, was a most peculiar dream. In it, Magda had come into my bedroom and moved to my bedside. I knew that it was her, yet there was something about the form that was not my Magda. Roused from my slumber, I attempted to sit up in my bed, but some unaccountable force held me still. Nor was I able to speak or call out. Slowly, the form appeared to float over the bed and onto my paralysed body. Then, all at once, I experienced the most incredible sense of fatigue. It was as if my own body was being drained of its life energy. I remembered nothing else until I awoke the following morning when, upon attempting to rise, I actually collapsed weakly onto the floor of the bedroom where I lay until the entrance, sometime later, of the upstairs maid with a cup of tea. On seeing me upon the floor, the poor girl shrieked, dropped the tea and vanished.

Somehow, I managed to drag myself over to the long dressing mirror and rise to stare at my reflection. I was horror struck at my appearance. My face was as pale as a newly laundered sheet, and my nightshirt soaked with what appeared to be congealed blood. My terrified eyes noticed the presence of two small puncture marks in the right had side of my neck – just over the position of the carotid artery, that continued to ooze bright red tendrils.

At that point my valet came into the bedroom, saw my condition, froze in his step, crossed himself and croaked one word, "vampire", before turning about and hurriedly leaving the room. At this point, the strength in my legs departed and I collapsed upon the bedroom floor

For the next half hour I lay there both exhausted and weak, dimly aware of the movements in the household below and finally noting the crash of the front door then silence. I must have then swooned for my next conscious memory was of the afternoon sun streaming through the bedroom windows. Attempting to rise from his position, and finding that some strength had returned to his previously hapless body, I staggered to his wife's bedroom. There I discovered the bed not slept in and the room showing little evidence of recent occupation. A gradual further exploration of the entire house showed it to be empty of any other person.

My earlier feelings of concern and worry began to turn to a sense of dread. What inexplicable event had resulted in my sole occupancy of what had previously been a busy household? And, more to the point, where was my dear wife? I decided, should my returned ability of movement permit, to go immediately to Bascott Hall and confront Sir

Eldon. Although my departed strength appeared to be nearly returned, I knew that I needed to eat before attempting the journey. Making my way down to the kitchen I discovered that, although it remained unattended, the large oven still contained a degree of heat and that earlier preparations for the evening meal had resulted in a large pot of soup resting on a corner of the iron hob. Having consumed over half its contents, and my former condition much improved, I was able to saddle up one of the pair of horses I kept stabled at the Grange, and ride over to Bascott Hall, arriving in the late afternoon.

The construction of the Hall allowed for a north facing entrance that supported a most delightful southern terrace leading onto a well laid garden and statuary overlooking the lake. Facing away from the sun at all times, the north face of the imposing edifice had always resented a somewhat grim exterior. In the late afternoon, with the sun well behind the Hall, the effect was eerie. The numerous windows stared back as venomous black eyes while the huge stone mass of the building seemed to grow and envelope me like a massive dark shroud. Shaking off my sense of impending dread, I knocked at the huge mahogany front door and waited.

After some moments the door swung open to reveal Belton the household butler. On his former visits, he would normally have welcomed me and ushered into me into the house without more ado but, on this occasion, Belton barred my passage. In response to my earnest questions, I was peremptorily informed that Sir Eldon was not at home and, furthermore, neither was Magda. Further attempts to enter the building were denied by Belton who stated plainly that Sir Eldon had forbidden anyone from entering the house. I thus had little option but to leave. Now extremely concerned for the whereabouts and condition of my wife, I decided to visit the doctor who, I believed, might be able to throw some light on the matter. However, my hopes were misplaced. The doctor stated that he had not seen Magda for several days. When I attempted to engage the other upon the marks on my own throat, the doctor brushed them off as possibly the bite of a rat while I slept, which was commonplace in country properties. My dilemma, both upon the disappearance of my beloved wife and the reason for the state of my own condition increased. Who might I turn to?

In desperation I sought out the local vicar. The Reverend Bennett had obtained the living at Dedham through the good graces of his Great Aunt Enid de Buys, and had ministered to the small, but God-rearing community for the past forty years. Now nearly 70 years of age, he looked forward to a few quiet years of well-earned retirement. His single pleasure consisted of reading novels concerning the criminal elements in the society of the day and, as such, had obtained and copiously studied the stories published in the Strand Magazine by a certain Doctor Watson.

Night had fallen by the time I reached the vicarage and knocked on the front door. Concerned by my distressed condition, the Reverend Bennett immediately ushered me into the small sitting room and poured a large glass of port before enquiring the reason for such a late evening visit. Briefly I told my story and was able to notice a distinct change in the other's behaviour when I mentioned my curious dream of the preceding night, and the physical state that I had found himself in upon waking that morning. Bennett became agitated to the point of nervousness. His eyes flitted about the room from door to window as if expecting another visitor. When I drew back my shirt and revealed the marks on my own throat, the gentle old cleric drew back and uttered a sound of pure terror, crossed himself and cried hoarsely. "Merciful God preserve us all".

Taken aback and further shaken by this sudden outburst, I attempted to press the old man for an explanation and it was from Bennett that I learnt the possible reason for my current condition. I became suddenly very afraid. What might I do? Who would help me if help were possible? It was then that Bennett had spoken about Holmes and yourself, doctor. Whereas you might be unable to provide for my spiritual safety, your physical presence would possibly ensure my personal, earthly protection.

I leapt at this suggestion and decided to leave immediately for London, but Bennett wisely counselled that, as darkness had fallen, I should remain at the vicarage for the rest of the night where, with the vicar's assistance, I would be safe. Bennett fetched a small tumbler of water and blessed it. Then, leading me to a guest room, sprinkled the contents of the tumbler on and around the room's single window and, further, the door and its architrave. Bennett also produced three silver crucifixes. One he inserted into the window catch, another upon a small silver chain he placed about my neck. The third, he instructed me to insert into the handle of the door to the room after he Bennett, had left.

I confess that my senses were reeling but I attempted sleep. At some period during the night, I vaguely remember a gentle knocking on the window – followed shortly by what sounded like a sharp hiss. But exhaustion overtook any possible fear and I slept soundly until the morning sunlight streaming through the window roused me and my previous terrors returned. Shortly after 8.00 a.m. I was able to catch the morning express to London and arrived at your rooms just before luncheon. Discovering that neither Holmes, Mrs. Hudson nor You were in residence, I stopped a passing hansom cab, obtained a scrap of paper and a pencil from the somewhat aggrieved cabbie, and pushed the paper through the front door. Thank God you discovered it.'

Brinton had finally arrived at the end of his tale and, for a few seconds, neither of us spoke. It was I who finally broke the silence.

"It is indeed a most curious account my dear fellow" I began, but Brinton leaned over and grabbed my knee with such force that I momentarily drew back in my chair. "You don't believe me do you Doctor Watson? My God, I am doomed". With that he dropped his head into his hands and stared helplessly at the carpet.

I was genuinely concerned for the poor chap and attempted to assuage his current fears. "Come, come old chap" said I, "I'm sure what you have told me is exactly what had occurred, but I need to speak with Mr. Holmes before we decide what we may best do to alleviate your current distress". Brinton brightened and raised his head. "Then you will help me?" he whispered. "Of course, my dear fellow" I replied, "but first let me get you another drink". Brinton gratefully accepted my offer and I noticed that some colour had returned to his previously ashen countenance.

Not knowing the exact movements of my dear friend, I placed Brinton in a small hotel just north of Piccadilly with instructions that he should lock himself securely inside his room, keep the window closed and fastened, and await the arrival of Holmes and myself as soon as I was able to contact the former. As no-one but the vicar knew of Brinton's trip to London, I felt sure that no harm would come to him that night. Whilst at the hotel, and booking Brinton in for the night, I spoke with the manager, with whom I had more than a nodding acquaintance, requesting that he, personally, serve his guest an evening supper within his hotel bedroom, and further instructed him to let no visitors into Brinton's room until I returned. This he agreed to without questioning my motives.

Quite sure in my own mind that Brinton's security was assured for the present, and after Brinton was safely locked in his hotel room, I remembered that I had promised an old friend living locally, and suffering an onset of peculiar symptoms, to call and spend a little while examining his current condition. Although my visit was not long, and my prognosis simply a case of gout, it was not until just before the hour of ten o'clock that I returned to my lodgings.

Chapter Two

Arriving back at Baker Street I noticed that our rooms were well lit, signifying Holmes had returned. Making my way quickly up to our lodgings, and declining Mrs. Hudson's kind offer of a light, late supper, I discovered Holmes apparently fast asleep within the confines of his favourite chaise-longue. I moved over and gently prodded his right arm. "Holmes" I said softly, "wake up my dear fellow." His eyes flicked open.

"I was not asleep Watson," he muttered somewhat peevishly, "merely resting my eyes and examining my thoughts. The brain tends to function far more satisfactorily when the eyes are less distracted by the images they normally view." He sat up abruptly. "You appear to be in some haste. Pray inform me what brings you home in such a rush".

"A most terrible thing my dear friend," I babbled, and my garbled words obviously contributed to my friend's further annoyance, for he stopped me sharply.

"How many times must I remind you Watson," he ordered. "Words to be correctly understood, and thus interpreted to convey the meaning in which they are intended, should be spoken precisely and distinctly. Calm yourself, I beg you, and begin again."

I sat down and began the story of my encounter with Brinton and the most distressing circumstances leading to his meeting with me in London. Holmes listened intently as I recounted the events in Suffolk yet, when I mentioned the word "vampire," he suddenly leapt to his feet, his eyes blazing.

"Good Heavens!" cried Holmes, "where is this man Brinton now?"

"At the Wilton Hotel," I replied.

"What!" Holmes's next words were almost a scream. "You left the poor wretch unattended, and at night? Do you realise what you may have done?"

My countenance dropped at his outburst and, seeing this, Holmes calmed considerably.

When he next spoke, his words were more moderated. "I'm sorry my dear old friend. I realise that your former actions were well intended. Please forgive my most uncommon and misplaced outburst. You could not possibly be expected to understand the dire peril within which this Brinton may now be placed. We must leave immediately for the Wilton Hotel and pray to God that we may still be in time."

Holmes picked up his top coat and threw it about his shoulders, then stopped and turned to me with a questioning look. "Do you have such an object as crucifix? he enquired.
I shook my head lamely. Holmes shrugged and made for the bookcase, selected a small black bound volume and thrust it into a pocket of the coat. "A bible will have to do then" he hissed. "Come Watson, we must be quick".

We left our lodgings, were fortunate enough to hail a passing hansom cab and, within a quarter of an hour, drew up before the brightly illuminated façade of the Wilton Hotel. Holmes peered out of the window of the cab and started visibly. "My God, I fear we are too late," he groaned, "come Watson."

We left the cab and made our way quickly into the foyer of the hotel. I noticed that a black police carriage stood in front of the entrance and that several uniformed constables stood nervously in the foyer. My acquaintance, the manager, leaned wretchedly on the hotel reception counter but said nothing.

One particular constable recognised Holmes and hailed my friend. "Oh, Mr. Holmes, thank Heavens you've arrived. It's not good sir. Not good at all."

"Which room is he is?" snapped Holmes.

"124, sir," replied the other. "Inspector Lestrade is already there."

Making our way to the room in question we found a young, ashen faced constable leaning limply upon the door jamb to the room. Behind the police officer a pool of vomit glistened wetly on the corridor carpet. The young man indicated weakly that we should enter the room, which we did. We then stopped dead in our tracks at the ghastly scene which confronted our horrified eyes. The room contained a single bed – upon which lay the dead body of Brinton. The corpse lay twisted in its final agony. Its eyes stared, fixed in the terror that must have accompanied the final moments of life. Yet it was not these features that attracted our dread attention. It was Brinton's throat – or what was left of it. From the chin to the shoulders a huge dark, bloody maw gaped blackly from where a neck should have conjoined the two. In fact, so terrible was the ghastly wound that the head itself remained attached to the body by the thinnest of sinews only.

Holmes gasped softly, and his jaw tightened, whereas my stomach heaved in revulsion at the terrible scene before us. I noticed Lestrade standing pale-faced in a corner of the room, as if unwilling to come any closer to the bed and its contents. Seeing us, Lestrade moved over and spoke solemnly.

"A terrible business, gentlemen, a most terrible business."

Holmes shook himself. "What time did he die?" he asked between tight lips.

"About an hour ago as far as I can deduce," replied Lestrade. "A porter heard him cry out, but the door was locked, and he had to summon assistance to break it down. I've got my men looking for the creature what did it. It won't get far."

"That is where you are wrong Inspector" said Holmes softly. "I fear that the creature to which you refer is long gone."

Holmes looked at the window of the room. It was open. "Who opened that?" he snarled.

Lestrade answered. "I've already checked that with the hotel staff," he said rather importantly. "Apparently, the chambermaid came into the room around 8.30, noticed that this poor fellow here was asleep and opened the window to let some air into the room. "She's innocent, you have my word on it".

Holmes turned on Lestrade. His eyes glared. The other shrunk back. "Innocent she is not Inspector. Her thoughtful act of opening the window let in the foul creature that did this." Holmes indicated the ghastly form upon the bed.

"Begging your pardon Mr. Holmes," said Lestrade, "but surely the creature has to be a large dog. Nothing less could have caused that damage. I've checked with the hotel staff and none of them has seen a dog leave the premises. It must still be here, and we'll get it. You mark my words."

Holmes looked sadly back at the blood-soaked corpse upon the bed. "I have to tell you Inspector Lestrade," he said, "nothing on four legs did that." Lestrade looked at Holmes with a puzzled expression. Holmes walked over to the bed and, for a few moments, studied the gaping wound. He then straightened up and rejoined us. "There is no more that may be accomplished here," said Holmes. "Come Watson, we have work to do".

Holmes turned to leave, and I to follow him, when Lestrade spoke again. "Do you have any idea who or what killed the poor fellow Mr. Holmes?"

Holmes nodded grimly. "I believe that I do Inspector. But I shall require time before I am certain."

"What do you want me to do with the body?" enquired Lestrade "will you require to examine it again?"

Holmes shook his head. "No, I have seen enough" he replied "you may remove the remains to the mortuary. Good night Inspector." With that, Holmes turned on his heel and walked out of the room. I nodded to Lestrade and followed him.

Our journey back to Baker Street was made in complete silence. It was obvious to me that Holmes was lost in thoughts of his own and I, in return, had little to say. Upon reaching our rooms, Holmes browsed his bookcase and brought out a leather-bound volume, opened the book and began to study. I poured myself a large brandy and offered Holmes the same, but he waved me away and continued to read. It was some half hour later that Holmes closed the book with a loud snap and looked up at me, his eyes gleaming. "We must go to Suffolk first thing in the morning Watson," he breathed.

"Suffolk?" I queried. "May I enquire for what?"

"To seek out and destroy a nest of creatures so abominable that to do absolutely nothing would definitely allow the further growth of a vile plague that, unchecked, might possibly imperil the whole of England," he replied.

"I'm not sure I understand you Holmes," I began, but he silenced me with an impatient gesture.

"Vampires, Watson. The undead spawn of the devil himself. I am certain that a hellish coven of these abominable creatures exists, most possibly at Bascott Hall. We must destroy every one of them before they, in turn, destroy us."

"Vampires?" I chided Holmes. "But they are creatures of legend. They don't exist. Come Holmes, you cannot be serious!"

Holmes's face was set hard. "I may never be more serious my old friend. Poor Brinton's story and tonight's events force me to believe that legend has become fact.

"Believe me" he continued "we shall be placing ourselves in terrible danger. Not only to our physical bodies but to the possible eternal damnation of our very souls. Yet, what has to be done must be done." At these words, Holmes relaxed somewhat and smiled at me.
"Now, Watson, I believe I might take a glass of that brandy if you please. I consider that we shall be in no danger this night for the evil creatures which caused Brinton's death should have, at present, no inkling of our involvement. However, tomorrow will be a different matter. We shall take the express to Colchester and, from there, travel to Dedham and on to Bascott Hall."

Holmes suddenly yawned then looked at the large ornamental clock on the fireplace mantle. "Good Lord, it's nearly one o'clock," he mused. "Right, Watson, time for bed. We shall need a good night's rest. It may be our last chance for the coming days."

Chapter Three

We arrived at Liverpool Street railway station at precisely 8:45 the following morning, and Holmes purchased two first class tickets to Colchester. I had thought that we might arrive earlier, but my friend insisted that we visit a local vicarage and then make a couple of stops on our way from Baker Street. The first was at a pawnbroker just south of the city and the other at a small timber business close to the station. Holmes had disappeared into both establishments, carrying a large carpet bag which grew in size following each visit. When I attempted to enquire as to what he had purchased, Holmes told me he would explain everything during our journey to Essex.

We had hoped to leave London on the 9 a.m. express but were informed by a member of the station staff that a cow had earlier wandered onto the railway line just outside Chelmsford and collided with the 7.45 slow train. It was thus that we finally departed from Liverpool Street station at 1.30 p.m. I had rarely seen Holmes so agitated by our delay. He kept muttering to himself about sunset and darkness and only ceased his perturbations when I purchased a cup of tea from the station buffet.

My friend had requested a reserved compartment and, as the express would its way slowly through the east end of the capital, Holmes closed the sliding door and sat down facing me.

"Now Watson," he murmured, "it's time for explanations. I thank you for your silent tolerance of what, to you, must have been most unusual actions on my part. Yet your very silence has allowed me mentally to prepare for what may lie ahead for both of us."

At this juncture, Holmes got up, took down the bulging carpet bag from the luggage rack and, after fumbling amongst its contents, withdrew the book he had read in our rooms the previous night. Replacing the carpet bag, he sat down. "What do you know about the subject of vampirism?" he enquired.

"As I said last night, I believe it to be the stuff of legend," I replied. "Mind you, I know that certain bats attack and suck the blood from sleeping cattle in parts of South America. They are, I believe, referred to as vampire bats. Apart from that, I know little else."

Holmes interrupted me. "Not just bats, Watson. The cult of vampirism extends also into the world of humans, though I confess that to refer to any of these satanic creatures as human is most sorely misplaced. Let me tell you of what I have been able to deduce so far."

Holmes opened the book, thumbed several pages then handed the open volume to me. I looked at the page and a sense of unease flooded my conscience. The lithograph that stared back from the page showed a man clad in a black cape. The eyes in the illustration glared malignantly back at me and the open mouth of the figure showed two incisors inordinately long, and from which dripped long trails of what could only be blood. I hastily handed the book back to Holmes. "Good Lord Holmes, what a dreadful drawing," I said, "What artist's fiendish imagination might conjure up such an apparition?"

"Fiendish it may be my old friend" replied Holmes "yet possibly no apparition. The creatures we are bent upon destroying may, indeed, resemble that picture."

I became silent – and Holmes continued.

"It is generally believed that the dreadful cult of vampirism originated in eastern Europe, although garbled accounts exist suggesting the filthy practice has existed since early times. Basically, a vampire can satisfy its dreadful hunger only on the blood of living humans. The creature, itself, is dead. Yet, because of its evil nature, may not enter what we refer to as heaven. It is thus undead to all intents and purposes, forced to roam the world of the living for all eternity. It fears the sunlight since exposure will destroy it. Thus, its hunting for blood must be confined to the hours between dusk and dawn. The active vampire possesses the strength of ten men. It may pass through solid doors and scale tall buildings with the agility of a monkey. Firearms do not affect it. To all intents and purposes, nocturnally the vampire is virtually indestructible."

"You said 'virtually indestructible,' Holmes," I interrupted, "then even in the hours of darkness, it may be destroyed."

Holmes shook his head sadly. "Not destroyed but repelled," he said. "It is said that holy water, fresh garlic and the presence of a crucifix are wholly repugnant to the creature. The only way completely to destroy a vampire is to drive a wooden stake through its black heart. Holmes stood up and again brought down the carpet bag. He tapped the outside of the voluminous article and smiled slightly.

"On our way to the station earlier, I obtained a flask of holy water, some silver crucifixes and a quantity of strong, sharpened stakes. I had hoped to reach Bascott Hall today before sunset and, thus, rid the world of these vile creatures, for I truly believe there are more than one. However, our delay has upset my plans.

"We shall, therefore, take accommodation in a local hotel for the night and resume our quest tomorrow morning. Even if the vampires know of our impending visit, they will be unable to do anything about it."

"How so?" I queried, "surely we shall be in danger the moment they discover our intent."

Holmes shook his head again. "A vampire may not enter a closed room unless he is invited by someone in that room. I assure you we shall be perfectly safe."

Holmes's words mollified my current concern for our immediate safety, but did little to suppress my interest.

"How are these creatures created?" asked I. "Do they breed as normal human beings?"

Holmes shook his head again. "As far as I can deduce, there appear to be certain host vampires who create their own covens and territories in which he or she, the senior member retains total control."

"There are female vampires?" I enquired.

"Most definitely" answered Holmes. "In fact, I believe that poor Brinton's wife is one. The party at Bascott Hall, and her overnight stay, were quite possibly her initiation ceremony into the hellish cult of vampirism. It all fits precisely – think of her daily lassitude and preference for darkness following that overnight stay. Brinton's discovery of his wife, and her condition within the grounds of The Grange, and his dream and subsequent frailty – together with the bite marks on his neck, convince me that Brinton was, himself, the object of his own wife's blood lust."

My interest was still aroused. "But you have made no mention of how these vampires reproduced Holmes. How does that occur?"

"The original host vampires may be hundreds of years old for, unless they are destroyed in the manner I have outlined, they are for all intents and purposes, immortal. In fact, many of their hellish converts may also share advanced age. Their reproduction, and I detest using a human expression when referring to inhuman creatures, is effected by their bite."

Holmes picked up the book again, found the page he sought and handed it to me. The open page showed the same drawing that he had previously indicated. "You will note that the incisor teeth are extraordinarily long Watson. With these, the vampire obtains the nourishment required by biting the victim's neck and sinking those terrible fangs into the carotid artery."

"But, surely Holmes, puncturing that great artery would cause death from blood loss."

"No, Watson" replied Holmes, "there appears to be a substance within the vampire's saliva that acts as a massive coagulant, sealing the wound after the creature has satiated its hunger. This allows the vampire to return to the same victim after the poor wretch has had time to replace the lost blood. Eventually the victim will die, but it is not death as we would understand the meaning. During the period when the vampire is feeding from his quarry, substances other than the coagulant are transferred by the vampire's saliva into the victim. Upon the victim's mortal demise, he or she, in turn, becomes a vampire."

"But then poor Brinton is now one of these awful creatures," I began, but Holmes stopped me.

"No, Brinton is really dead. Of that fact I am certain. In attempting to seek your assistance he sealed his own doom. He knew too much and was, obviously, of no further use to the Suffolk coven. The horrendous wound you saw in Brinton's throat is known as the vampire's death bite. Even accepting that Brinton may have been the unwitting victim of an initial attack by his wife, insufficient quantities of that dreadful serum would have been implanted into his blood stream to ensure his eventual transformation onto that most unholy state. Whatever, and whoever, killed him would have known that fact. I truly believe that Brinton may now rest in peace."

"But how did they know of Brinton's visit to London?" I enquired. "Apart from his earlier visits to the doctor and the local vicar, he saw no-one before he met me."

"Obviously we may discount the vicar," replied Holmes. "However, the doctor may be another matter entirely. We must be on our guard against that gentleman."

Holmes took out his meerschaum, lit it and began to puff, and I sensed that our conversation was now concluded. I must have dozed off, for my next recollection was of my friend's gentle prod to my arm.

"Colchester," he remarked. "We're here".

Chapter Four

Enjoying the reputation as England's oldest recorded town and, furthermore, a Roman provincial capital before London, Colchester is served by the River Colne, from which trade between it and the metropolis is a busy daily occurrence. The railway station is situated north of Colchester itself, and access to the town necessitates travelling up a steep hill at the summit of which may be found the main High Street.

I confess I had never before been to Colchester and the sight of such a bustling community that sunny afternoon did much to dispel my earlier trepidations and forebodings. In fact, both Holmes and I were in quite the merriest of humours when we booked overnight accommodation at the Three Cups hotel. The hotel itself is quite as grand as some of our London hostelries and our rooms furnished beyond critical comment. According to Holmes, the last Bourbon King Louis XVIII rested here overnight before his return to France at the fall of Napoleon.

As there were several hours before dinner, Holmes and I decided to explore the town. At the eastern end of the High Street we discovered the famous castle. Built by the Normans on the site of an earlier Roman temple that, itself, had been destroyed by Boadicea in A.D. 60, the castle stood grandly within its own grounds.

"It contains the largest Norman keep in all England," remarked Holmes.

I was astounded at my friend's innate knowledge.

"My God, Holmes," I exclaimed. "How on Earth did you know that information?"

Holmes smiled broadly and winked at me. "It's contained in this pamphlet I picked up at the hotel Watson," he replied, producing a folded piece of printed paper and waving the same before my wondering eyes.

"Oh Holmes, you play with me cruelly," I said, but the merriment evidenced within the eyes of my friend would not allow me to become annoyed. "Here am I, believing you to be one of the cleverest minds in all England, and now I discover that such previously evidenced brilliance may, in part, be purloined from pamphlets!"

At this remark, Holmes cocked his eye and adopted a most superior countenance. "One of the cleverest Watson" he said. "You are sadly mistaken in that respect – I am the cleverest." Then he laughed. "Come on my old friend, it is nearly time we dressed for dinner."

It was thus, and in the most genial humour, that we returned to our hotel. We ate promptly at eight o'clock in the large, chandeliered dining room of the hotel. I confess I was mildly surprised at the selection of courses offered by the chef which would not have been out of place in a large London restaurant. Having decided upon native oysters, beef consommé, turbot and mutton with potatoes and seasonal vegetables, we then considered the hotel's most expansive wine list. Holmes initially ordered a bottle of Château Latour Martillac 1887 and a further bottle of

Château Margaux 1885 with the mutton. Both wines were excellent.

As the dining room was appreciably full of evening diners, we avoided any conversation on the matter of our visit to Colchester, and contented ourselves with naught but pleasant and innocuous banter.

Holmes suggested we should retire at a reasonable hour and, by ten thirty, I retired to bed and fell instantly asleep. The night was mild for the time of year, and the hotel bedroom stuffy. I had opened one of the large double windows to allow some ingress of fresh air. In my innate sense of well-being, conditioned by the admirable meal I had recently consumed, I ignored the caution I should have exercised, and my act in attempting to gain some fresh air placed me in a most dangerous situation.

I must have been asleep for about an hour or so when something caused me to wake. I realised I had failed to extinguish my bedside candle before nodding off, and was about to remedy this omission when a soft sound caused me to look towards the bedroom windows. There, in the dim gloom, my horrified eyes beheld the most hideous apparition. I could see it was a man, although the indistinct figure evidenced little sharpness of outline. He was completely bald and his face glowed with a whitish-yellow luminosity, unaffected by the dancing flame of the flickering candle. The apparition began to float slowly across the room floor to my bed. It was then that I saw its eyes. Black rimmed circles from which emanated the very fires of hell itself bore into mind. I tried to look away, but some invisible force held me in its fiendish grip and, although my instinct was to get away from this horror, my limbs were frozen, and my will dissipated by those terrible orbs. The dark, fat lips of the face parted, revealing two sharp white incisive daggers protruding some half an inch from the other teeth. The figure reached my bed and bent over me and my senses were assailed by the vile stench of bloodied corruption upon the creature's breath. Closer and closer the face dropped to my throat, and my brain screamed in frozen terror.

Suddenly my bedroom door flew open and Holmes rushed in. The figure by my bed whirled and hissed and the spell in which I had so recently been held evaporated. I threw myself from my bed and staggered towards Holmes who, himself, had halted for an instant and drawn back on seeing the abhorrent dreadfulness of the creature before him. Then, gathering his senses, Holmes raised his right hand in which he held a silver crucifix and cried in a firm voice. "By God and all his Angels, I command you to depart whence you came, foul abjured spawn of hell."

With that, Holmes threw the contents of a small flask that he held in the other hand, over the monstrous abomination that still crouched upon the bed.

The effect of this action was instantaneous.

The creature shrieked and clawed at the areas upon which the contents touched. Its form contorted in pure agony and horrible, smoking, suppurating sores, blotched its vile features.

Suddenly, as though pulled by an invisible rope, the vision flew backwards from the bed and out of the window into the night sky.

Both Holmes and I said nothing for a few seconds. Then Holmes turned to me. His face was ashen – although, when he next spoke, his words were controlled. "That Watson is what we are set against," he said quietly.

"But how .....?" I began, and Holmes pointed to the open window.

"There, old friend. There is its means of access to you" he said. "I blame myself in failing to warn you earlier. An open window is as much an invitation to these vile creatures as if you had requested their presence."

"But how did you know I was in peril?" said I.

"I heard your call" replied Holmes.

"But I didn't! I said. "I was unable to move or call out so strong was the influence of that fiend."

"Yet I did hear you," said Holmes. "You, or something, spoke to me." Then his face adopted a look of wonderment. "I believe the Powers of Light may have interceded on our behalf this night, Watson. If that is the case, then we have powerful allies in our search for these foul denizens of hell."

"Powers of Light? Whatever are you talking about Holmes?" I enquired innocently.

"I will explain in the morning," replied Holmes. "For the present, I believe we shall both be safe for the rest of the night and should try, as best we are able, to get some sleep."

Holmes walked to the bedroom window, closed the open one and hung the silver crucifix onto the catch. He walked to my door and turned back to me. "Just in case" he murmured. "Just in case." Then he left the room and closed the door quietly behind him. I must have been totally exhausted by my recent experience for, no sooner had I laid my head upon the pillow, I fell into a deep sleep and remained so until the maid arrived with coffee at seven o'clock the following morning.

The bright early sunlight dispelled much of the terrors of the previous night and it was with a light heart and a growing appetite that I made my way down to breakfast. Holmes, already seated at the table was busily scanning the pages of the early edition. He looked up, folded the paper and smiled briefly as I entered the breakfast room. "Watson, my dear chap. How are you?"

"Fully recovered," I replied quite brightly. "In fact," I continued, "I'm beginning to think that last night was just a dream."

Holmes's face tightened. "Be sure that it was not my dear friend," he said quietly, beckoning me to take a seat beside him. "I am afraid that the events of last night were all too real and allow us both an indication of what awaits should we persist with our investigations into this infernal situation." He looked about the breakfast room and, perceiving several other guests, looked back at me. "We'll speak about this matter later during our journey to the

Hall," he continued. "Now," and he brightened up considerably, "I'm for the kippers".

An hour later our hotel account settled, and following Holmes's somewhat protracted financial negotiations with a local coach owner, our hired horse and gig made its way at a merry pace along the High Street, down the steep hill that led to the road to Dedham, and into the countryside.

The morning sun was hot and this, together with the rhythmic clop of the pony's hooves and the gentle sway of the gig induced in me a delicious torpor of contentment. I fell into a snooze in which I fancied myself on a wondrous magical carpet floating over a palm-filled desert. My carpet descended and beneath me I saw a tent from which came forth the most beautiful creature who, seeing me, beckoned my presence. Nearer and nearer I floated, my total attention fixed upon her coal black eyes which promised pleasures beyond imagination. Then, softly, her soft lips curled back revealing sharp white fangs. In my dream I sought to draw back, but was compelled – as by some inestimable force – to draw closer. I screamed and in my delirium heard the voice of Holmes.

"For goodness sake Watson, wake up!"

I shook myself awake. There was no carpet. Just the jolting of the gig and Holmes looking at me curiously.

"You were asleep," he murmured, "but behaving rather peculiarly. I thought I'd better wake you up."

I was about to recount my dream but felt better of it. In any event, the glorious countryside did much to expunge any memory and, by the time we reached the hamlet of Dedham, I had completely forgotten the whole matter.

"I think we should make the acquaintance of the local doctor as our predominant duty" said Holmes. "After that," he continued, "we must call upon the vicar."

The local inn produced the doctor's address as a rather large house at the far end of the village. However, upon our arrival there, we were informed by a woman, whom we deduced to be the housekeeper, that Doctor Gresham was out. A dark green gig stood parked in front of the house and, noticing this, Holmes enquired if it belonged to the doctor and, if so, whether he was within. The housekeeper appeared somewhat reluctant to answer this question – merely stating that the doctor had employed the services of another vehicle that day and was not expected back until the following morning.

Leaving the doctor's house, we travelled to our second place of call – the vicarage. The small, rather pretty, cottage stood behind the church. Yet again, there appeared to be no-one at home, the door being firmly closed and remaining so following our repeated knocking.

"Where is everybody in this hamlet," groaned Holmes. "We seem to have picked a day when Dedham is deserted."

As he uttered these words, a man appeared around a corner of the church. Well past his prime, and sporting a veritable halo of white hair he, nevertheless, was wearing a cleric's collar and was, obviously, the local vicar.

Noticing the man, Holmes called out. "Good day vicar. A moment of your time if you please."

The vicar stopped abruptly and stared at us. I noticed a weariness in his eyes, bordering on fear.

"My name is Watson, my dear fellow, and this," I added indicating Holmes, "is Mr. Sherlock Holmes. I believe you have heard of us." A look of relief rose upon the old man's face and he managed a smile, walked towards us and offered his hand.

"My dear Holmes, let me introduce myself. I am Oswald Bennett, the vicar of this parish," he mumbled, taking my colleague's hand and pumping the same quite vigorously. "I see Brinton has contacted you." At this, the old gentleman looked about questioningly. "But where is Brinton?" he enquired.

"I think it would be more appropriate if we discussed the matter within the confines of your vicarage" said Holmes. I noticed the former look return to the old man's eyes but, without further words, he guided us into his house and ushered us into the small, but quaintly furnished, living room.

"May I offer you some refreshment?" he enquired. "Perhaps a glass of sherry?" Without waiting for our reply, he poured out three generous portions and handed Holmes and me a glass each. "Now," he said, "what of Brinton?"

"Dead," responded Holmes.

"Merciful Heavens!" cried the horrified cleric, "How so?"

"His throat was torn out by someone or something in London," replied Holmes. "The police believe it was the work of a stray dog, but I think both you and we know better ....."

At these words the vicar crossed himself, closed his eyes and muttered a silent prayer. "Then it is true" he whispered. "When Brinton first came to see me, and appraise me of his terrible tale, I suspected as much."

"If you refer to the existence of vampires within this small community," said Holmes softly, "then I fear you are correct. More to the point," he continued, "I believe the lair of these foul abominations is situated at Bascott Hall. "

"You say 'these abominations' in that you infer there may be several," queried the clearly shaken cleric. Holmes nodded gravely.

"From what Brinton told my friend at their initial meeting, and from events which have subsequently occurred, I believe there may be a virtual coven of the hideous creatures," he replied. "But, surely, there must perforce have occurred other seemingly inexplicable incidents within your parish which would suggest such a vileness exists."

"There has been talk of the disappearance of one of two village girls," said Bennett. "But in these rural communities young girls are always running off to the big cities in search of gainful employment, and little long-term attention is paid to such disappearances."

"Ah," sighed Holmes, "now, what about inexplicable deaths, reported sightings of a dead person, marks on an injured throat?"

The old vicar shook his head slowly. "I see little of the living as it is" he began. "My parish, although large by accepted standards, contains, to the greater extent, country folk who although by no means of an atheist persuasion, find little time within their accepted – yet strenuous – existence, to attend my services. In fact, few summon my attendance when, at the end of their lives, preferring only that my presence be forthcoming upon their interment. So you see, Mr. Holmes, I fear that any information I may be able to provide on your question may be of little practical value."

"But surely the local doctor will have knowledge" said Holmes. "For I fear that Brinton's death is but one act of a series which has occurred as the result of the existence of these vile creatures. If one associates the emergence of the vampire with this region approximating with the occupation of Bascott Hall, then for the past year or so many unfortunate souls must have fallen foul of their inexorable lust. Has the doctor not said anything to you that might cause you concern?"

At these words the old cleric looked sharply at Holmes. "The doctor? You've met the doctor?"

Holmes shook his head. "No, we called on him but were informed that he was out and would not return until possibly tomorrow."

A strange expression appeared upon Bennett's face – whereas his actions became furtive. "Be careful of that individual," he murmured. "He has only resided in the village for some twelve months, yet already there are certain stories emanating within the community."

Holmes was immediately interested. "Stories," he repeated. "What stories?" Noticing the vicar seemed loathed to say anything further, Holmes prodded him. "Vicar, it is of the utmost importance that you tell me exactly what has been circulating about this doctor. Tell me everything. Leave nothing out."

The aged cleric stood up and refreshed our glasses before answering Holmes. "You must understand that what I am about to tell you is the pure hearsay of others," he began. "I, for myself, will have nothing to do with the man and he, in return, keeps well away from my vicarage. However, shortly after he took up residence here, a local labourer was heard to say that he had observed the doctor within the confines of his own parlour, apparently praying before a table, upon which stood black candles and an upturned crucifix. At the time, little attention was paid to the man's rambling story since he, himself, was a known local troublemaker and had witnessed the event of which he spoke, while returning from an exceedingly jolly evening at the local inn."

"Were you not yourself concerned about the man?" enquired Holmes. "After all, if the labourer's tale were true, our Dr. Gresham would, by all accounts, appear to be a practising Satanist. Surely that would be a matter for the Church?"

The old vicar shook his head sadly. "I am no longer young Mr. Holmes," he said quietly. "At my age, the soul is strong but the spirit weak. Rather than possibly confront the power of the Devil, I meekly accepted the labourer's story as the fanciful ramblings of an inebriated known troublemaker, and did nothing."

"Tell me!" said Holmes, and his voice took on an air of command. "How well does the doctor know Sir Eldon?"

"Extremely well, as far as I can deduce" replied Bennett, "his carriage has been seen and noted on numerous occasions at Bascott Hall."

Holmes leapt to his feet, his eyes blazed. "That's it" he hissed.

"What is?" I enquired somewhat lamely. Holmes turned on me.

"Don't you see, Watson," he said harshly, "it all fits, Gresham is Eldon's familiar."

"I don't follow you," I said. Holmes ignored my interruption.

"Vampires need a servant or, in this case, a familiar, who is not of their own physical state, yet who may be relied upon to carry out such necessary tasks that the vampire itself may not undertake. What better for the vampire, being the spawn of Satan, that he obtain the services of a follower of that cursed fallen angel? It all fits."

Holmes then clapped his hand to his head. "My God," he cried out. "The doctor may be with his evil master at this very minute. He whirled upon me. "Come Watson, we must be away immediately if we are to put a stop to the vile business."

Holmes turned to Bennett and his voice dropped to a more conversational tone. "I must go to Bascott Hall and attempt to destroy such creatures as are there. Whatever occurs, I shall return here before dusk. If I fail in my objective, both my colleague and I shall require such protection as the church is able to provide this night, for any surviving vampires will, I feel, launch attacks upon the hated precursors of their destruction."

With those words Holmes hurriedly quit the vicarage, leapt into the gig and whipped up the horse. Luckily for me, I remain blessed with a certain nimbleness; otherwise, I am sure Holmes would have left me behind.

Bascott Hall lay some three and a half miles distant from Dedham, and on the road to the neighbouring hamlet of Ardleigh. The Hall, itself, was reached by a long drive, fronted by large iron gates. A steep hill confronted us as we left the outskirts of Dedham, which slowed our pace somewhat and, thus, it was some twenty-five minutes after we quit the village that the entrance to Bascott Hall hove into view. We had not suspected any trouble other than when we entered the Hall, and were correspondingly startled by the three men who stood menacingly by the main gates.

"Curses!" exclaimed Holmes. "I did not expect that we might receive the attentions of a welcoming committee. Do you have with you that monstrous firearm, Watson?"

"Of course," I answered.

"Keep it ready," instructed Holmes. "For the present, avail yourself of one of the stakes that I have brought with us."

I did as my colleague suggested and Holmes drew the carriage to a halt some ten yards from the assembled men, and called out to them. "I presume you men are employees of Sir Eldon Manning," he said. "If that is the case, be so kind as to open the gates for I have urgent business with your master."

The largest of the three men said something to the others and, together they moved towards the carriage. I was able to see that all three carried large cudgels within their clenched fists.

"Drat," hissed Holmes. "I fear we are about to be set upon by these ruffians. Watson, your pistol if you please. Perhaps the sight of a firearm may dissuade these fellows from what blatantly appears to be their intended course of action."

Hearing Holmes's words, I quickly sought inside my coat jacket and produced my heavy revolver I always carried when with my colleague on business. The effect was instantaneous on the three other men. They halted and drew back a pace or so.

"See 'ere yer honour," he said addressing me. "Now there be no need fer that. We don't want no trouble wiv ye. It's all our job's worth to let ye into the manor when his lordship 'imself don't permit it."

So intent upon the three had I been that I failed to notice there was a fourth man who had concealed himself in the bushes which bordered the road. I relaxed my grip on my pistol slightly which possibly saved my wrist being broken by the stroke from the previously concealed other. As it was, I suddenly felt a gigantic blow to my arm and dropped the firearm into the roadway.

With a roar of unconcealed triumph, the four of them launched themselves at our carriage. Yet, quick as they were in their assault on us, they were wholly unprepared for the speed of Holmes's reaction. Practically before the eye might blink, he had drawn his sword-stick, buried its gleaming three-foot length of naked steel within the shoulder of the nearest ruffian and withdrawn the same. The man shrieked with pain and reeled away from the carriage clutching his injured shoulder. The others, shocked by the ferocity and speed of our retaliation, stopped dead in their tracks.

"Quick Watson," cried Holmes, leaping from the carriage and advancing threateningly upon the remaining thugs. "Be so good as to pick up your pistol and follow me."

I did as I was bid but found there was little need for the additional protection since it became obvious the villains who had sought to injure us, were in no mood for the type of retaliation that had occurred. With various curses and expletives, they hurriedly made off, dragging the injured man along the road, and in the opposite direction from which we had arrived.

"I believe that is the last we shall see of those rogues," said Holmes. "Now, let us make haste for I fear this delay may have cost us valuable time in our attempt to deal with the evil which inhabits this place."

"How on Earth did those fellows know of our coming," I enquired.

"The attack on you last night evidences the fact that he, or they, know of our presence in the area Watson," replied Holmes. "If I have surmised correctly, the part Dr. Gresham may play in this matter, I fear these vile creatures may have been already warned, and steps taken to ensure that we fail in our mission. However, we must go on."

With that, Holmes opened the large wrought iron gates, resumed his former seat in the gig and whipped the horse into a gallop over the long drive which led to Bascott Hall. As we drew up in front of the large grey stone edifice, I was able to see the great entrance door hung open wide. Of any sign of life, there appeared to be none. To all intents and purposes, Bascott Hall was empty. There was even no indication of the presence of Gresham's carriage.

"Curses," hissed Holmes, we are too late".

Nevertheless, he instructed me to collect stakes, garlic and several of the small crucifixes from the large travelling bag and, together, we speedily entered the vast building.

"Spare no moment in seeking our prey in any other location than a cellar," said Holmes. "It is daylight and the darkest place in this awful structure is where the vampire will be discovered."

It took us little time to find the entrance to the cellar of the Hall, and even a shorter period in which to see that whatever had been concealed within its cavernous, dingy confines was no longer there. All that remained were several wooden trestles.
"Confound it!" cried Holmes, "the coffins in which they should rest before they awake and continue their foul search for sustenance have gone. The creatures are out of their lair."

"What do you propose we should do now" I enquired.

Holmes took out his gold Hunter watch and studied the face of the timepiece. "We may do little here" he said tersely. "It will be dusk within an hour or so, and the last thing we should do now is to remain here. I feel we should immediately return to the vicarage and make such preparations as we may against any attempt on us during the hours of darkness. Come Watson old friend," he added, "let's be away."

Chapter Five

The evening sky was bathed in a most glorious sunset by the time we arrived back at the vicarage and it was difficult to imagine what possible horrors awaited the both of us in the following hours of darkness. The vicar, obviously terrified at the evil within his community had, nevertheless, spent the time while we were away in examining what steps he might take to preserve our joint safety and, following discussions with Holmes, it was agreed that we all should spend the night within the confines of the parish church, it being the holiest structure in the area.

"According to my researches into the current, little accepted evil," said Holmes, "a vampire cannot cross consecrated ground."

"However," he added, "that is not to say that he, she or rather it, may not attempt to reach us this night. I fear we must prepare for the worst." He turned to me. "Watson, be good enough to pass me that carpet bag," he requested, indicating the object he had placed near the door to the parlour in which we all sat.

I did so, and Holmes opened the bag and then addressed the vicar. "I have with me crucifixes and a flask of holy water" he began. "I suggest we immediately place the crucifixes across any and all points of ingress to your church. I assume you also may be able to provide additional crucifixes should we require them." The frightened vicar nodded lamely.

"I also believe you should straightaway prepare further quantities of consecrated water so that we may be sufficiently supplied should the need arise" continued Holmes.

"I have already prepared quantities of the same while you were away," replied Bennett.

"Excellent," said Holmes. "Now, what we appear to lack is garlic or, more precisely, garlic flowers?"

"Garlic flowers," said I.

Holmes nodded. "From my recent researches into this vile culture, it is suggested that a vampire may well be repelled by the presence of the plant. Whether this is a fact or not, it will do little harm to avail ourselves of sufficient quantities if we are able to procure them."

"I am certainly able to assist you in that area," interrupted Bennett. "During my time in India as chaplain to the 14th Bengal Lancers, I acquired a taste for the rich curries of that country and have always cultivated the plant. In fact, there is an abundant supply within my own garden at this very moment."

"Excellent," said Holmes again.

Moving over to the room's small window he scanned the sky for a moment and muttered, "The sun is nearly set." Holmes picked up the carpet bag and spoke to Bennett. "Take Watson with you and collect the garlic" he commanded. "We must immediately repair to the church and install such items that are necessary for our salvation this coming night, for I fear it may not be too long before we face our first assault."

Within five minutes we had gained the sanctuary of the holy building, securely fasted the heavy door and set out the crucifixes and garlic as Holmes directed. "There would appear to be no stone left unturned," remarked Holmes, standing back and examining the result of our joint efforts. He turned to Bennett. "I believe, vicar, you should now conduct what prayers you are able for the safety of our mortal souls."

The vicar nodded and moved to the altar where he knelt and began a series of incantations which were inaudible to both Holmes and me. We waited and, after several minutes, the vicar rose and came over to us. "It is done," he said simply. "However," he added, "should all else fail, there exists an exultation which may be used only if the soul is in mortal danger. It is the ultimate cry for spiritual help and, thus, should never be used lightly for fear of the terrible and irreversible results if used wrongly."

"I see," muttered Holmes. "Then pray to God we shall have no use for it".

It had been decided that one of us should attempt to get some rest while the other two kept watch, and it fell to me to be the first to try and sleep which, unsurprisingly, was of little problem. I was, therefore, a trifle annoyed when woken by a nudge from Holmes.

"Come on old chap," chided Holmes gently, "you've been fast asleep for nearly three hours. It's time for the vicar's nap."

"What time is it?" I enquired shaking myself awake.

"Shortly before eleven," replied Holmes. Suddenly he froze and stared at the church door. He held up his finger for absolute silence. Then I distinctly heard the noise. It was the soft scrape of a shoe or boot on the threshold outside. As we stared at the door there came a gentle knocking from without and a voice spoke.

"Reverend Bennett, are you in there?" said the disembodied voice. We all said nothing, and the voice spoke again. "Reverend Bennett, I need to speak with you. Please let me in."

Bennett turned to Holmes and spoke in a hushed whisper. "It's him. It's the doctor" he hissed. "What shall I do?"

Holmes moved quickly over to the heavy door. "Go away" he commanded. "You are not welcome here."

There was a brief silence and then the voice spoke again. It was more aggressive this time. "Who are you?"

"I am Sherlock Holmes."

"I am Gresham, the local doctor," said the voice. "I need to speak with the vicar. Let me in."

"If you are indeed Gresham," cried Holmes "then you should realise we know of your foul association with those vile creatures at the Hall. Get you gone for I shall be after you come the morning light. Of that you may be most assured."

I swear that then I heard a hoarse cackle for outside the door the voice spoke again.

"Morning?" it croaked. "By morning you will either be dead or slaves of the Master, Mr. Holmes".

"Be off, you foul abomination," shouted Holmes. "Neither you nor those vile creatures you succour shall enter this holy place this night. In tomorrow's light, I shall personally commit each one of you to the hell you deserve."

There was no response to my colleague's outburst and, after a few moments, it was plainly clear that Gresham had departed.

"That was their first attempt," said Holmes quietly. "But," he continued, "I fear not their last." Turning to the ashen faced Bennett he said kindly "Come vicar. Try and get some rest. Watson and I will stand guard for the next few hours." Bennett settled himself in one of the pews and was soon snoring quietly.

"I will let him sleep until morning," whispered Holmes. "But what of you?" I whispered in return.

"I have no need of sleep my old friend," replied Holmes. "I need to be awake and ready at any time through this night." He looked about the church. "I think I will take a circuit of the place," he murmured "just to ensure myself that such preventatives as we have already installed are in their correct positions." With that he stepped away and began moving about the building.

I had never been in a church, virtually on my own and at that time of night, and the illumination by such of the candles we had lit, cast flickering and quite disturbing shadows upon the stone, timber and glass that surrounded me. Was that a figure standing beside the vestry door? What was that movement beside the altar? My imagination began to run riot, and I longed for the companionship of my friend's return. Suddenly I knew for certain that my imagination was not playing tricks. I distinctly heard the sound of soft scratching. My eyes searched wildly for the source of the sound and focused upon the large stained-glass window which stood above the altar and there, in the reflected candle light, clung a shape which resembled human form. Horror struck, and I cried out.

"Holmes, where are you? Come quickly."

"I've seen it Watson," came my colleague's quiet yet firm voice and, spinning around, I realised he had heard and come to stand at my side.

"What are we to do?" I whispered.

"More to the point," replied Holmes "what does it intend to do?"

We watched silently as the scratching continued. Then, suddenly, a single pane of the leaded glass few inwards and the shape of a hand thrust its way through the created aperture. By the slightest chance the outstretched claw collided with a line of garlic flowers and immediately withdrew from the window's opening. The hand's disappearance was accompanied by the most ghastly scream of frustration and rage I had ever heard, and the shape disappeared immediately from the stained glass. Silence returned.

Holmes was the first to react. "Quick Watson. We must seal that opening," he shouted. "Whatever was outside has created a breach in our defences which must be closed immediately."

Moving quickly to where we had left the ladder with which we had previously positioned our earlier defences, Holmes placed it against the window wall and began to ascend. "Hand me one of those spare crucifixes," he commanded. Then, clutching the item, he climbed quickly up to the point where the glass had been displaced, and wedged the silver piece within the remaining aperture. He climbed down and surveyed his work.

"Well, the garlic appeared to work," he began. "Yet, for the life of me, I cannot understand how the creature was able to cross holy ground. Poor Bennett must be mistaken in that area. "Unless that is," he added, "these fiends are able to cross consecrated soil as long as their vile bodies make no contact with the ground."

"Will they come again?" I enquired nervously.

Holmes shook his head. "Of that I am unsure," he replied. "Obviously, they are now informed of our previous defensive preparations. Whether or not these barriers may be breached by a force against which we have no defence, I cannot be certain. We shall have to wait and see."

"So, there is nothing else we may do to protect ourselves," said I.

"No," replied Holmes. "In fact," he continued, "I believe we should spend such time as we are able in discussing what further course of action we adopt, should we survive this night unharmed."

We discovered the presence of several chairs which were obviously to be used in the unlikely event that all the existing pews were filled, and further seating required for the congregation. Holmes positioned two of these chairs facing each other in the centre of the aisle. This allowed the both of us to watch a section of the church while we conversed. After we had decided that our joint vision would allow us to survey the entire interior of the building at a single glance, Holmes began.

"With the coming of sunrise, the vampire will lose its power and be forced to return to its place of unhallowed rest," he began. "We may thus assume that we are safe from further harm during the hours of daylight. Therefore, initially, I believe our first action should be against the doctor. It is he, I believe, who was responsible for moving the carcasses of those abominable creatures away from the Hall, and to their current place of unhallowed safety. This is why we discovered his own vehicle parked by his house. He must have used a far larger means of transport."

"What do you intend we should do?" I enquired.

"Obviously, he must be destroyed" said Holmes. "Yet any action upon my part which may be proved to have caused that damnable creature's death, may well result in a murder charge on which I would have little defence."

"But the man's a Satanist, and in league with vampires" I began.

Holmes waved me to silence. "Satanism, or rather covert Satanism, is not a punishable offence in this enlightened world" he began. "And any mention of the existence of creatures generally accepted to be figures of fiction would be taken as the ravings of a lunatic. However, although the man must be stopped or, at the very least, put away in a place where he is unable to offer any further assistance to his foul master. I now consider our prime action to discover the resting place of the other creatures and their utter and complete destruction."

"But we have no knowledge of their whereabouts," I began.

Holmes held up his hand. "But the doctor has," he said emphatically. "That is why we need him to lead us to the other creatures."

"He will hardly do that of his own accord, Holmes," said I.

"That is precisely why I feel he should not be apprehended," replied my colleague. "Should he wrongly believe that he has avoided our attentions, he is bound by the loyalty that he owed his wretched Master to oversee the safety of that heinous coven.

"At first light," he continued, "we shall pay another visit to the doctor's house. He will not be there I am certain, yet we may be able to deduce some evidence of his possible whereabouts from his housekeeper."

"What if we fail to discover the vampires tomorrow, Holmes?" I enquired.

Holmes looked drawn. "I fear we may not," he replied softly. "But if we can attract their attention, it may spare some other poor soul from their foul ravages. We know that, within the limits of this church, we enjoy a degree of safety as may be deduced from tonight's occurrences, and I truly believe this sanctuary may continue to exist for any coming nights we are forced to endure before our mission may be accomplished. However, during the hour or so, I have been giving the matter some considerable thought, and I feel that someone in authority should now become involved. Someone" he added "with legal authority who might be able to bring the force of law or, at least, sanction our proposed actions against both these vampire creatures and Gresham."

"You have this someone in mind?" said I rhetorically. Holmes nodded sagely.

"Lestrade. He has already seen what damage these creatures are capable of and, although I am sure that, initially he has about as much belief of the existence of these creatures as he does in the existence of the Philosopher's Stone, he nevertheless is a man of fact. I, therefore, propose to telegraph the man tomorrow, at our first opportunity, and request his presence in Dedham at his earliest convenience. Which, knowing Lestrade as I do," he added, "will be later in the day. In any event," he concluded, "should we be attacked again tomorrow night, it will give the man practical experience of what we are asserting is, in fact, correct.

"That is precisely why I must return to Colchester at first light," he muttered. "Both you and the vicar will be perfectly safe whilst I am away, and I should be back in Dedham by mid-morning. During my absence," he continued, "I would be obliged if you would make enquiries from anyone who offers vehicle for hire within the hamlet. I doubt that Gresham possesses two vehicles. Therefore, he must have obtained the one in which he travelled to the Hall, locally."

"And Gresham? What of him?" I asked.

"I doubt if the wretch will be anywhere to be found come morning," replied Holmes, taking out his gold Hunter, studying the face and then looking up at one of the church windows, from which could be seen the pale light of the coming dawn.

"Ah," murmured Holmes softly. "I note the peril of the recent night is now passed. I believe we now may awaken our clerical friend." With that he gently woke Bennett. "Come on old chap. You can wake up now. We're safe for the present."

With Bennett fully awake, Holmes quickly appraised the old fellow of our earlier discussions. The vicar, it appeared, knew of a local resident, a man named Offord, who regularly offered his Hackney for hire, and I was despatched to seek out this individual while Holmes made his way, post haste, to Colchester.

Chapter Six

It was but a short walk to Offord's yard, and I found the fellow both at home and of a most genial and pleasant disposition. Yes, he possessed a Hackney carriage and, yes, the doctor had employed its services the previous day. Offord gladly showed me the vehicle which occupied a corner of his yard. It was only at this juncture that some of his former geniality seemed to vanish.

"Look," he said rather sadly. "What a condition to return a rented vehicle."

I had to agree with the man. The carriage was caked in what appeared to be clotted sand. The bright paintwork that glowed briefly from the uncovered areas, was, elsewhere, slurred with rusty-yellow streaks.

"Dunnow where he's been to get all that sand?" continued Offord. "There ain't much of the stuff around these parts."

Our immediate conversation was suddenly interrupted by the sound of a horse's hooves, followed by the appearance of a young lad leading a horse.

"Brought the gelding back, Mr. Offord" said the lad. "Dad says it'll be sixpence for the new shoes."

"And where does your dad expect me to find that sum of money?" said Offord smiling and winking at me. "Alright young Charlie," he said, turning to the boy, "Give me a minute, and I'll get your dad his money."

"Don't let me hold you up any longer, my dear fellow," said I, moving away. "I have to be off anyway. However, my colleague may wish to speak with you further upon his return from Colchester."

"Always here," said Offord cheerily and waving a salutary hand.

I left and returned to the vicarage to find Bennett still within the church. The old gentleman, still clearly fearful from the experiences of the previous night, seemed unwilling to leave the place which had been our sanctuary. My reassurances seemed of no avail and, although I was loath to leave the poor man, I began to feel extremely famished and decided to attempt to avail myself of some breakfast at the local hostelry.

Assuring the old vicar that I would return within the hour, I left the church. The Sun Inn is situated some 70 yards from the church in which we had spent the previous night. It is a pleasant hostelry which bisects the main high street, offering simple, yet nourishing, fare to the passing traveller. Of custom, the place appeared bereft, yet the cheery landlord willingly offered me a plate of delicious Suffolk sausages and fried potatoes which I consumed with rapidity quite inappropriate to a gentleman of my station.

Having finished my meal, I was making my way back to the church when my attention became riveted upon the green gig which stood outside the doctor's house and, more to the point, the figure of a man who was climbing into it. I broke into a run and reached the vehicle and grasped the leading trace. The man turned to me, his face contorted in anger.

"Gresham?" I cried out.
The other's eyes blazed with demonic fury. "Yes," he hissed, "what of it?"

"Get out of the gig," I ordered. Gresham's eyes narrowed. "Why?"

"I was in the church last night," was all I said. The other appeared visibly shaken, although his demeanour remained unaltered.

He cackled. "So, you are still alive."

"No thanks to you and that vile tribe who you serve," I replied. "Now get down from the gig."

"Move away, curse you," snarled Gresham, raising the heavy whip which he clutched in his right hand.

My own hand sought and found the heavy revolver within the deep pocket of my overcoat. I began to draw out the weapon, but Gresham was too quick for me. With a scream of fury, he brought down the whip onto my arm and whipped the horse into a furious gallop. I staggered back clutching my injured arm, and watched as the doctor sped away down the street. He turned and screamed at me "The rest of you will be dead by tonight!"

Had the doctor taken more interest in the roadway along which he fled, he would have noticed the low, sweeping branch of an old yew tree which lolled across his path.

But he did not. The thick sinew caught him squarely upon the side of the neck and hurled him from the gig and into the roadway, where his twisted body sprawled grotesquely. My inherent training as a doctor overcame my revulsion for the man, and I hurried down the road to the inert body and stooped to examine the same. It was of little use. The man's neck was broken and a pulse extinct. Gresham was dead.

Having assured myself that this was so, I sought about for some assistance to remove the corpse from the street. A wagon was coming slowly down the road and I hailed the driver. The cart pulled up. The wagoner slowly alighted and came over to stand by the body. "Best we get him to a doctor" said the other.

I shook my head. "I am a doctor," I replied, "and, I am afraid this man is beyond all human help. However," I continued, "I believe we should remove the body from the roadway and transport it to a place where it may be left while the relevant authorities are informed. May we use the facilities offered by your wagon?" The other nodded and, together, we lifted Gresham's corpse onto the wagon.

"Where do you want to take him?" enquired the wagoner.

I considered this question for a few moments before replying. "If you will wait here, I will approach the landlord of the local inn, and he may have an outhouse and, if agreeable, allow us to leave the body there," I said.

"I got a delivery to make," he replied, "but it can wait."

Hurriedly I made my way back to The Sun. The landlord, although at first somewhat wary, agreed that Gresham could be placed for the time being, in a small outhouse, until preparations were finalised to move the corpse elsewhere. With the space of three quarters of an hour we had moved Gresham's corpse and the wagoner departed.

With Gresham safely deposited, at least for the present, I made my way back to the church. As I reached the little pathway leading to the main door I stopped short. There was something wrong, something terribly wrong. The entrance door lolled partially open. The open door did not, by itself, cause my sudden sense of impending dread; it was the pool of red upon the entrance flagstones that glistened wetly in the morning sunlight. I moved to the doorway and there beheld a sight that froze my senses.

The vicar lay on his back, his arms outstretched as upon a cross. His eyes stared sightlessly at the vaulted ceiling beams. His mouth a frozen rictus of astonished terror. The altar crucifix inverted, protruded from the remains of his smashed ribs while uncongealed blood oozed in heavy rivulets from the ghastly wound and crawled in crimson tendrils across the church floor. I had witnessed sudden death on many occasions, yet the awful savagery and indignity of Bennett's demise caused me to stagger back and clutch at the church door for support. My senses, reeling as they were, I nearly suffered a heart attack upon hearing the voice which spoke at my back.

"Steady, Watson."

I whirled about. Holmes stood a scant pace away, lips pursed and grimly surveying the ghastly scene. "Holmes," I gasped. "Thank God you have returned."

Gently taking hold of my arm, Holmes guided me out into the morning sunlight. "I cannot understand it," I mumbled, still badly shaken. "I was only away from Bennett for about an hour or so."

"The doctor," hissed Holmes. "It must have been he."
"But the doctor is dead," I began.

Holmes interjected. "What!"

"I've just carried his corpse to an outhouse beside the inn," I continued.

Briefly I explained to Holmes the events of the past few hours. Holmes listened intently until I had completed my story. "The vile beast must have carried out this dreadful deed while you were at breakfast," he muttered. "You are sure he is quite dead?"

I nodded. "His neck was broken quite clean through," I explained. Holmes was lost in thought for the next few seconds. Then he spoke again.

"The doctor's demise cannot have occurred at a better moment," he began. "For, without his assistance, those abhorrent creatures are deprived of any mode of transport from wherever they now lie. Although they may rise to roam at will during the hours of darkness, they will be forced, from now on, to return only to the place where the doctor laid them."

"But we do not know where this may be. The doctor was our only hope of determining their whereabouts," said I.

"That is true," said Holmes. "Yet what you have told me concerning the condition of the hackney used by the man in furtherance of his vile deeds, I believe an examination of the detritus coating the wheels and body of the vehicle, may prove positive in identifying an area wherein the creatures rest. We must pay a visit to your friend Offord at once."
I glanced back to the terrible sight that I knew waited inside the church. "What of poor Bennett?"

"I believe we should leave everything untouched," replied Holmes. "As far as I can recall, there is a key in the inside lock by which we can ensure nobody may enter that building until Lestrade arrives at some time this afternoon.

"He is coming?" I interjected. Holmes nodded.

"It would seem that Lestrade was in his office on the arrival of my initial telegraph," he said. "He replied immediately that he would be here later today. He also intimated that he would be bringing others with him." His serious features betrayed the semblance of a grin. "I am unsure to what extent the members of the local constabulary will feel their territory has been invaded by outsiders, nor do I care." He indicated that I should then accompany him back to the church, where we managed to close the heavy door and lock the same without recourse to moving the vicar's body. "Now," said Holmes defiantly. "Let us go and see Offord."

Fortune appeared to smile on us that day as, upon our arrival, we discovered Offord, due to other commitments, had not been able to clean the vehicle concerned and it, therefore, remained in the condition in which I had initially viewed it. Holmes examined the carriage in minute detail and, after some time, returned to the spot where I was attempting to glean as much information on the recently deceased local doctor as I might. Little, it appeared, was known of either the man or his habits, and the conversation had turned to the most welcome assistance of the wagoner in dealing with the initial disposal of the corpse.

"He's a good man," remarked Offord. "Always ready and willing to do someone else a good turn, whether it's carting a load of bricks for old Ned in the village, or hauling those big blocks of ice up to the Hall.

"What did you say?" said Holmes, who had arrived after completing his inspection.

"Pardon," said Offord.

"About blocks of ice and the Hall."

"It's for the ice house," replied Offord.

"Which Hall?"

"Why, Bascott Hall. There ain't no other Hall in the area."

Holmes's eyes gleamed with interest. "And where in the Hall is this ice house?" he asked impatiently.

"Oh, it's not in the Hall," replied Offord. "As far as I can recollect, it's over on the far side of the estate. Near the Manningtree Road."

"Manningtree" mused Holmes.

"Little place down by the backwater," offered Offord. "You can't miss the ice house if you take the Manningtree Road and follow the wall of the Bascott estate until you get to the turn off to Manningtree. It's just past there; sort of huge mound in the ground. Holmes was definitely excited by this information.

"Tell me" and his question was very nearly a scream. "What would the soil be composed of in that area?"

"Sandy," replied Offord. "Folks say there is a seam of it that runs from off the estate right down to the coast. Wait a minute," he continued, and a puzzled frown creased his features. "That could be what's on my hackney. If it is," he continued, "whatever was the doctor doing over at the ice house? Mind you," he chuckled "might be the best place for him now in his present condition." His attempt at black comedy was lost on my colleague.

"That's it," hissed Holmes turning to me. "Come Watson, we have little time." And then, to Offord, "My dear fellow, please forgive my somewhat hasty departure after your most valuable assistance, but I have just remembered I am due at a meeting, and any misplaced tardiness on my part will not be accepted lightly by he whom I must meet."

Offord, obviously unused to the verbal delicacy of this form of departure, merely gaped, touched his forelock and nodded. We left and made our way along the High Street in the direction of the church.

"That's where the creatures lie," said Holmes defiantly. "That swine Gresham must have removed them from the Hall and into the ice house. He pulled out and studied his Hunter. "It is now just before the hour of two in the afternoon," he continued, "my telegram to Lestrade was received at around nine o'clock this morning. Assuming the man caught the first available train to Colchester, we may presume he will arrive in that town somewhere around one o'clock. Allowing sufficient time for him to procure the services of some form of transport," he mused, "I expect he will be with us in Dedham within the next half hour or so. Come on old friend," he added taking my arm, "let us get back to the vicarage."

Chapter Seven

As always, Holmes's deductions were incredibly accurate for, twenty minutes later, a black police vehicle hove into sight at the far end of the main street, made its way slowly along the thoroughfare until it reached the church, and stopped. Lestrade's figure emerged from the confines of the van, followed by several other men in ordinary dress, and four uniformed police officers.

"Capital," breathed Holmes, making his way over to the Inspector and positively grasping the yet un-proffered hand of the other. "You've come."

"I answered your telegram," said Lestrade. "You said my attendance was urgent. That was enough for me, Holmes. But, for the life of me, I fail to understand the urgency of your earlier communication."

"Thank God you have come," said Holmes shaking Lestrade's had forcibly.

"Steady on Holmes," replied the other, somewhat taken aback by the intensity of my friend's greeting. "Your telegram told me to be here as quickly as I could, so I caught the first train available. What's up?"

"More than might be explained in a few moments, my dear fellow," replied Holmes. "What has happened already and, moreover, what I believe might well occur shortly, certainly warrants the attention of one of the more intelligent members of the police authority."

"And you sent for me?" answered Lestrade – and I swear the man's chest heaved with unconcealed pride. "But I'm only an Inspector," he added modestly.

"What matters rank or position to me," stated Holmes. "It is the professional competence of the man that I value above all other" he continued "and that is why I sent for you". Lestrade actually beamed with satisfaction."

"Then I am entirely at your disposal," he replied.

"Then I suggest we remove ourselves straightaway to the scene of what I consider a most foul murder," said Holmes. "And if my deductions prove correct, the crime, itself, is but secondary to an act you, yourself, have previously witnessed."

"What!" stammered Lestrade.

Holmes waved him in the direction of the church. "Come see for yourself, after which I will explain everything."

We made our way to the door of the church and Holmes pushed open the heavy door. Lestrade peered inside and, upon seeing the mortal remains of the vicar, pulled sharply back.

"Poor bloke," he grunted. "Looks like he was carrying the thing and then slipped and fell on it,"

Holmes grimaced. "I hardly think so," he remarked acidly. "No simple accident would effect such penetrating injuries. Someone, or something, thrust that crucifix into the man's body. Of that fact, I have not the slightest doubt."

"If you say so," mumbled Lestrade. "But who did it?"

"I believe I know," said Holmes. "But, before I disclose that information, I must necessarily speak with you privately and advise you of a state of circumstances I am sure currently exist, and my own deductions thereupon, the telling of which may cause you to doubt my own sanity. However," he continued, "I assure you that I am in perfectly sound mind, yet the evidence I shall shortly produce, and my own conclusions upon the same may, I fear, tax your own abilities to accept a situation that, in our present enlightened times, remains within the realm of folklore and legend."

Lestrade's eyes narrowed. "Hang on, Holmes, what's all this about my abilities?" he began, but my colleague ignored his interruption.

"Permit me to advise you more fully within the confines of the vicarage," he chided softly, taking the other's arm and guiding him in the direction of the late vicar's abode. He turned to me. "Watson, be so good as to instruct the uniformed constables as to their positions should we require their presence this coming night."

He turned to the plainclothes officers. "You gentlemen should repair to the local hostelry and there attempt to obtain lodgings." I was about to reply but Holmes and Lestrade had already entered to vicarage.

With Holmes gone, and the plainclothes officers away at the local hostelry, I busied myself instructing the uniformed police in, what I believed, should be their duties during the coming night. They were all big fellows and appeared somewhat amused with my instruction that they were to work in pairs.

"Don't see the need for us to patrol with a mate," said one. "We're big enough to cope with anyone on our own."

As I could hardly describe the creature that had attempted to enter the church the previous night, I contented myself with explaining that whatever we might expect would quite possibly be of some considerable physical strength. This seemed to mollify the policemen.

"Must be a bloody monster," said one, and the rest giggled. Sadly, his remark might not be closer to the truth, yet I kept my mouth shut.

Fortunately, both the northeast and southwest corners of the church allowed uninterrupted vision of all sides of the building and it was at these intersections that I instructed the uniformed officers to take their positions. Several yew trees allowed a degree of protection for inclement weather, should it occur, without obstructing the general view of the surrounding ground, while the pervading seasonal warmth would permit a night of sufficient comfort for the men outside.

I had completed issuing my suggestions for the night's vigil to the uniformed officers, when I noticed Holmes and Lestrade had re-appeared from the vicarage. The latter looked ruffled.

"You mean to tell me I have come down from London on what appears to be some cock and bull story of creatures that are, to all intents, figments of historical legend?" said Lestrade. "Really, Holmes? I would have thought better of you."

Holmes's face was set. "You really must grant me the respect due from our earlier cases together Inspector," he said acidly. "You should realise by now that I am not in the habit of embarking on flights of fancy. If I tell you that a certain situation exists – it does."

"But what should I put in my reports?" enquired Lestrade somewhat plaintively. "I can hardly state that what you have recently explained to me is a murder, was due to the act of a creature of legend. I'll lose my pension".

Holmes smiled briefly. "You may forfeit a great deal more than your pension should you agree to remain here this coming night my old friend," he said. "That is," he continued "should you fail to appreciate the terrible danger we will all be in if we fail to take appropriate precautions."

Lestrade shook his head resignedly and sighed loudly. "Alright, I'll give you one night," he grunted. "If nothing has occurred by tomorrow morning, I'm treating this matter as a simple murder and, as such, my then investigations will proceed upon an accepted and normal basis."

"Capital," said Holmes. He nodded in the direction of the church. "I believe that, before we discuss our plans for the coming night, we should endeavour to remove the earthly remains of the late vicar to a more practical location. Would you agree Inspector?" Lestrade nodded.

"Good," said Holmes who then turned to me. "Watson, pray enquire whether the landlord might be prepared to accommodate a further body within the confines of his outhouse. You may inform the fellow that he will be adequately compensated for his trouble, and that both bodies will be removed tomorrow morning." Holmes turned back to Lestrade then, noticing that I had not moved, swung back to me. "Well, hurry up old man," he said anxiously. "We have but little time to prepare ourselves for the coming night as it is."

Initially, the landlord was at some pain to accept the arrival and storage of a further corpse, remarking somewhat glumly that he "ran a public house ..... not a bloody mortuary," but, after realising that his financial reward would quite possibly exceed a full night's takings, reluctantly agreed that the vicar's body might reside for the coming night within the confines of his outhouse. This being the case, a black humour briefly raised within me the thought that both murderer and victim should soon occupy the same shed. However, I put the thought from my mind and hurried back to the vicarage where the uniformed constables loaded the vicar's body into the black police van and made off to the Sun. The landlord, however, remained adamant upon one point. The overnight accommodation for the plainclothes men was entirely out of the question. Such rooms that were normally available having been already reserved for a party of water colour artists from Brentwood. I reported back to Holmes.

"If that is the case," said Holmes, on being informed of the situation, "then they shall remain with us in the church. Please return to the inn and endeavour to obtain sufficient blankets to afford us a degree of comfort during our vigil." This I managed to effect, although the landlord was none too pleased to release such items from his hotel and, more to the point, to gentlemen whom he barely knew, and who had the propensity to produce dead bodies for his storage.

Holmes appeared most concerned that the uniformed police officers remain outside the church. He approached Lestrade.

"You appear to have failed to grasp the evil forces that we are up against, Lestrade, if we are assailed this coming night, four men, let alone one, will be of no match for the power of evil that will come against us."

"Come on Holmes," chided the other, " My men are quite capable of looking after themselves. I would put one of mine against any other miscreant, attempting to come at us this evening."

Holmes gave up.

"Be it upon your own head," he replied wearily.

So, much against his better judgement, Holmes agreed to the situation. Holmes, Lestrade, the remaining plainclothes officers and I would remain inside the building until morning. As such artefacts as had been employed the previous night appeared to have been successful in warding off the previous attempts on our lives and souls, they would be re-used for our next nocturnal sojourn.

Holmes had decided to brief the assembled police, both uniformed and plainclothes, on the reason for their attendance in Dedham. However, for the present, he had confined the facts to the apprehension and arrest of a certain well-known individual believed guilty of the most nefarious practices. This appeared to satisfy all.

Chapter Eight

As it was still about a couple of hours before sunset, Holmes insisted that we all repair to the local inn where we might avail ourselves of a hearty meal before we faced such rigours as the night might impart. It was thus that we returned to the church as the sunset. The landlord of the Sun had grudgingly allowed us the use of some straw mattresses which we arranged somewhat precariously over the church pews, and which afforded those not upon watch, a reasonable comfort. Holmes had also insisted, but only after considerable resentment from the uniformed officers, that each wear a crucifix beneath his clothes and, after this was affected, the four policemen left to take up their assigned position outside the church, while we settled down within. Knowing the effectiveness of the plant against what might attempt to harm us, I had collected virtually armfuls of garlic from the poor vicar's garden which, to the amusement of the plainclothes officers, I placed around the building.

"Bit early for Harvest Festival," giggled one man, and it became obvious that both he and his colleagues had failed to appreciate the seriousness of the situation. From the earlier discussion with Holmes, Lestrade had privately briefed his officers, but it became plain for all to see that they, and he, were treating the entire exercise as something of a time-waster, but, as they were being paid for it and, more to the point, had recently enjoyed a supper far above their normal expense, were prepared to allow the situation to continue at least until the morrow.

The sun had set, and the night gleamed starkly through the latticed, stained window panes. Holmes had placed a veritable gallery of lighted candles within the building and the soft flickering of the silent flames lent a comforting glow to the stone arches and corbels that towered above us. The plainclothes men were engaged in a game of cards. Lestrade, who appeared intent on the contents of a small book, occupied a pew close to the door of the church, while Holmes and I busied ourselves in constantly checking the various artefacts we had earlier placed about the structure. As it is, when it is being watched, time passed slowly and without incident, and it was just after I had checked my watch – showing a little after the hour of ten o'clock that I thought I heard a soft scream from without the building. I was immediately alert and turned to Holmes.

"Was it .....?" I whispered.

Holmes nodded. "Yes," he hissed. "Be ready Watson".

We were standing close to the altar and at some distance from the main door, yet we both saw Lestrade suddenly rise from his seat and move towards it. "What are you doing?" shouted Holmes.

The inspector turned. "Someone's knocking to come in," he replied innocently. "I'm going to see who it is," he continued.

"Don't move," commanded Holmes, but it was too late for Lestrade had already reached the door and was in the process of opening it.

"Quick, Watson," cried Holmes, picking up a carafe of holy water and dashing to the door which Lestrade had now opened, and then stepped suddenly backwards, revealing the form of a young woman standing on the stone threshold.

The girl, for she cannot have been more than sixteen or seventeen, wore a rough peasant smock which had fallen from her shoulders to reveal a magnificent bosom, around which curled the lustrous tendrils of her raven hair. Her mouth was full and red-lipped and bore the semblance of a smile while her eyes were of the purest violet.

Lestrade stood riveted to the spot not more than a yard or so from the vision of loveliness, his mouth sagging with the awe that he obviously found in her perfection. Involuntarily, Lestrade took a step forward.

"Stop!" screamed Holmes.

At his outburst, the girl flashed him a quick glance, and suddenly her facial features contorted into a mask of pure evil. She drew back her lips, exposing two fangs of the purest white, snarled gutturally and launched herself at the transfixed detective inspector. Lestrade, caught unawares, tumbled to the church floor. The creature straddled him, her eyes now changed to red orbs of hate, her body bent forward, her mouth seeking the softly pulsing hollow in the other's neck. Lestrade screamed in pure fright while he strove to escape the dreadful embrace but, try as he might, it was clear that he was no match for the girl's strength. The creature uttered a hoarse cry of triumph as her mouth lowered itself upon the spot it so eagerly sought. But Holmes was quicker, and without shortening his pace, threw the entire contents of the flask onto the creature's back. The effect was immediate. With a ghastly scream of anger and pain, the girl's body snapped into a terrible rictus.

Wherever the droplets of holy water had touched became spots of smoking carnage and the church filled with a horrid sizzling noise. The creature rolled away from Lestrade, staggered to its feet and fled the church. Quick as a flash, Holmes shut and locked the door. For a few moments silence filled the entire building. Lestrade was first to speak.

"What the hell was that?" he muttered softly.

"That," replied Holmes tersely "that was a vampire. Perhaps you now believe everything I have told you so far."

"My God," said Lestrade shakily, "you saved my life Mr. Holmes."

The others were on their feet and stood awkwardly in a small group. It was plain for all to see that they were shaken and more than a little frightened at what they had just witnessed. Holmes addressed them.

"What you have just seen gentlemen," he began "is but part of the evil we face. I have to tell you that what we may soon encounter in our efforts to rid the world of this scourge, will place you all in far greater danger, but I see from your expressions that you no longer feel I have been wasting your time."

"What's happened to that thing?" enquired an ashen faced young detective.

"You have nothing more to fear from that creature," replied Holmes.

"She will have returned to her vile coven where her Master, seeing her ravaged features and realising that she can be of no further use, will probably destroy her with a death bite.

However," he continued, her presence here, gives illustration to you all of the enormity of evil, that we must surely soon face and destroy."

"Lead us to it Mr. Holmes," cried another detective who appeared to have recovered his senses. "We'll finish it tonight."

Holmes shook his head. "That is precisely what we shall not do" said Holmes. "Darkness imbues the vampire with extraordinary strength. Even the men here would be unable to capture and destroy what may await us out there. By day, the vampire must return to its resting place, and it is then and there that we shall put an end to this vile curse."

He stopped speaking and looked about him, then continued. "I am reminded of the police constables who were left outside to keep a watch. We must immediately see to their present condition, though I fear we may already be too late."

"What do you mean 'too late'?" enquired Lestrade.

"Oblige me with each of you taking a crucifix from the collection on that pew," said Holmes, indicating one of the benches. "I believe that now we have little danger in venturing outside, but it pays to guard against all eventualities." He turned to me. "Watson, do you still have your gun upon your person?" I nodded.

"Good" said Holmes, patting the breast of his coat. "I, too."

Lestrade and the other detectives needed no second bidding in the mad scramble to obtain the objects indicated, and thus it was but a few moments later that Holmes undid the heavy church door and, together, our party made its cautious way into the churchyard. Holmes carried a powerful torch, and it was a little time before we discovered the uniformed policemen, or rather what remained of them, at the north-east corner of the building. As Holmes's flashlight illuminated the forms of the men, I distinctly heard Lestrade's sharp intake of breath, followed by the sound of retching from a plainclothes officer.

Both uniformed officers lay upon their backs, their dead eyes reflecting the horror of their last moments before death mercifully closed their minds to further outrage. The bloody collars of their uniforms gleaming wetly in the beam of Holmes's torch, each man's throat had been torn out with a savagery beyond description.

"There's little we may do here," whispered Holmes. "Pray to God that the others may yet have escaped such a grisly end."

We made our way quickly in the direction of the south-western corner of the church, but of the two officers directed to guard this area, we found no sign. "Probably got fed up with the wait and buggered off," remarked Lestrade drily. "Lucky for them," he continued "otherwise they'd have ended up like their mates."

I noticed by the torchlight that Holmes's mouth was fixed in a grimace. "I pray you may be correct," he hissed. "But I am seized with a terrible fear that those poor fellows may even now have become part of the vile league that we seek to destroy."

"What the devil do you mean, Holmes?" enquired Lestrade somewhat angrily.

Holmes spun round upon him. "What I am trying to tell you, my dear Inspector," he said hotly, "is that I fear these men may now, in turn, become vampires themselves."

"But that's impossible" began Lestrade, but Holmes shut him up.

"Impossible," he hissed again. "Surely you must remember yourself how, but a short time ago, that creature easily rendered you incapable of offering any defence to her attack upon your body."

"What are you saying?" demanded Lestrade. "Surely, if these men were attacked by the same thing that did for their mates, they would now be as dead as their comrades."

"No" replied Holmes. "Though it would be merciful if they were so.

"I don't understand you Holmes," said Lestrade.

"Part of the foulness of these creatures is to cultivate converts to their vileness," began Holmes. "They accomplish this ghastly practice by ensuring their evil bodily fluids are transmitted by their saliva into the bloodstream of their victims through their bite." Lestrade's expression was uncomprehending.

Holmes continued. "According to my researches into this detestable creed, I have deduced that the vampire possesses two kinds of bite. The killer, such as was administered to the unfortunate fellows back there, and to Brinton in the London hotel; and the conversion bite which, although effectively causes the recipient to become spiritually dead, allows the unhallowed body to pursue its eternal quest for blood."
"My God," breathed Lestrade. "So, what you are saying is that the other policemen are now vampires themselves." He paused and shook his head. "What the devil am I saying?" he blustered. "You'll have me believing in things that are the grist of fairy stories. I am becoming as cracked as you are, Holmes." My colleague ignored this last remark".

"Have your men remove the bodies of the other men into the church," he instructed. "If my deductions are accurate, we shall have nothing to fear from them for the rest of the night. Once we are all safe within the church, I will attempt to explain to you and your men what we must surely effect on the morrow."

Following Holmes's directions, the bodies of the two policemen were removed from where they lay and placed within the small confines of the church crypt. Although my colleague believed they would cause us no further harm, the crypt door was locked, and a crucifix garlanded with garlic flowers placed around each dead man's neck, and the bolt to the door.

For the next hour Holmes lectured Lestrade and his colleagues on what he knew of the vampire and its behaviour. It was interesting to note that, whereas earlier, the plainclothes policemen had tended to regard any discourse on the subject as the ramblings of a crackpot, they now listened in rapt, nervous attention.

"The only way positively to destroy the existence of the vampire," Holmes concluded, "is by driving a wooden stake through its heart, removing its head and then burning the same to ashes. That is why," he continued, bringing out a most wicked looking, gleaming butcher's cleaver from an inside pocket of his top coat, "I carry this."
"But what you are proposing is nothing short of cold-blooded murder," retorted Lestrade. "How am I going to explain that to my superiors?"

Holmes looked grim. "Murder applies to a living human being," he replied gravely. "The thing that we must destroy completely, is neither human nor, for that matter, alive. It belongs to the realm of the undead."

"Alright Mr. Holmes," said Lestrade. "Just supposing, for the moment, that I accept what you are saying might just be true. But, it's a long way to convince others that any actions we may take to rid the world of these creatures may be anything other than cold-blooded slaughter on our part,"

"I've considered that aspect," replied Holmes. "It is, therefore, vital," he continued, "that any actions we may collectively undertake remain of the utmost secrecy."

Lestrade appeared mollified. "I agree," he muttered and, turning to the assembled plainclothes officers, raised his eyes for their affirmation. All nodded their agreement.

"Good," said Holmes. "Now, let me outline my plan of action. Bearing in mind the vampire may only roam during the hours of darkness, it is imperative that we commence any action against these creatures as soon as the sun rises tomorrow. I thought, originally, that these vermin of hell rested within Bascott Hall itself. However, I now truly believe they have been removed to the confines of the ice house which occupies a position on the eastern border of the estate. It is to that place we shall initially go upon the break of dawn." He took out his Hunter, looked at it for a moment, then replaced it inside his coat. "It is now just after two o'clock," he continued. "At my reckoning, we all have about four hours until sunrise. Therefore, I suggest we attempt to avail ourselves of some rest within the intervening hours. The travails we will possibly encounter on the morrow are certainly not for the tired mind and sluggish body. I will wake you some half an hour before dawn breaks, and ensure you all have with you the items required to destroy these creatures. Now, it is time for sleep."

I am certain that everyone within our small group managed at least a couple of hours' rest, for I did, and it seemed that my eyes had barely closed before I felt the gentle, yet firm, nudge of my colleague and heard him whisper, "Come on old friend, wake up, it's time".

I shook myself awake and stretched to alleviate the cramp which had seized my body from the night's uncomfortable rest. When we were all fully awake, Holmes delved into his large carpet bag and brought out the various items which were to assist our day's labour.

"I have three mallets and sufficient quantity of wooden stakes to encompass whatever we discover on reaching the ice house," he began. "Watson and I will take a mallet each. That leaves a spare." He looked about the gathered policemen and his gaze fell upon a burly, sandy-haired officer. He held out the spare mallet. "Wilson, you may have this. Some force may be required to drive the stake through the body of one of these creatures, and it may need the strength of someone of your build and stamina."

Wilson smiled and took hold of the mallet. "I'm your man Mr. Holmes," he murmured, "though, for the life of me, nothing in my training has prepared me for the things I may have to do today." The others looked at each other uneasily.
Lestrade intervened. "Are you certain this is necessary, Holmes?" he began. "If we discover these creatures, as you refer to them, might we not simply bind them and bring them back to secure cells within the local police station?"

Holmes whirled upon him angrily. "Good God man!" he riposted, "Do you still not realise what we are facing? The evil we must shortly encounter possesses the strength to snap any shackles we may place upon it. Placing any of the vile creatures close to a heavily populated community would only allow it to roam at will to satiate its inane lust for blood. The creatures must be totally and irrevocably destroyed. Furthermore, if such an action as you propose were physically possible, what charges might you seek to bring against them? As you have said already, this vile spawn of hell is, to most, merely a fantasy of story books. No! We must find this ghastly coven and despatch it back to the foul ungodly regions whence it came. If any of you require justification for the acts we must affect this day, think of those two poor officers who now lay within the crypt."

Lestrade nodded. "You are right, of course. It's just the thought of killing anyone goes quite against the grain of my training as an officer of the law."

Holmes's face was grim. "You must cease to regard these creatures as people" he began. "They bear as much resemblance to living human beings as the droppings of a dog in the street. Our failure utterly to destroy them all may release into the world such a plague of pestilence that the Black Death will appear as but a summer cold," He looked about at the assembled men. "Do you clearly understand what I am saying?" The others nodded and grunted their comprehension.

"Right," continued Holmes. "Each man will take with him a crucifix and a flask of holy water. For added protection," he added, "Everyone will wear garlands of garlic about their necks. That should ensure our safety should we encounter any of the vile monsters not constrained by the daylight hours, and who may seek to do us harm."

The others collected the items that Holmes had prescribed and, together, we all made our way to the black police vehicle. Holmes, Lestrade and I occupied the large front seat while the plainclothes officers took seats along the benches ranged along the sides of the rear. Holmes and Lestrade had jointly decided to allow the bodies of the unfortunate uniformed policemen to remain in the crypt until our return later in the day. Holmes excused himself and left our party for about half an hour, returning bearing several thick staves upon which were large bundles wrapped in what appeared to be reeds. "Torches, gentlemen," he proclaimed somewhat proudly. "It will be dark within the confines of the ice house, and we shall require all the illumination possible for the task ahead. Now, if we are ready, I suggest we make haste. The morning is well advanced."

Chapter Nine

It was at 10 o'clock precisely, that the black police van trundled along Dedham High Street, made its way out of the village and took the road to Manningtree.

The sun was high and the Suffolk countryside, lazy in the warmth of the day, drifted yard by yard past the jolting police van as it slowly made its way along the rutted road. It was easy for me to allow the same sense of contentment to slip slowly into my conscious senses that I had experienced on my initial journey to Dedham, yet my fear of what might await us at the end of our travel fought against the feeling that sought to invade my languid brain. Dimly I heard Holmes explaining to Lestrade the process of the destruction of the vampire.

"The stake must be driven precisely into the creature's heart and the wound sprayed with Holy Water," stated Holmes. "I do not believe the head needs to be severed, though it might be an added precaution if it is done. I intend that we should burn the bodies to ensure that nothing physical remains of this terrible plague."

"Good Lord, Holmes," ejaculated Lestrade, "what you intend is nothing short of the murder of who, to all intents and purposes, are innocent people, purely upon your own surmise that they are evil creatures of fiction."

Holmes looked at him sharply. "It would seem that your experiences of last night have failed to convince you of the existence of these vile creatures," he muttered icily. "What further proof do you require? Would you be more content if you were to witness one of these execrable demons slavering upon my own throat or that of Watson here?" The mention of my name brought me back to full consciousness immediately.

"What!" I exclaimed. "You mention something about a vampire and my neck. Have I missed something?"

Holmes chuckled. "Return to your reveries my dear chap, I was merely explaining to our friend Lestrade the absolute need for the complete destruction of the entire coven of these creatures as and when we come upon them."

I was immediately mollified. I turned in my seat and tapped Lestrade lightly on the shoulder. "You must believe everything Holmes says," I began. "I, perhaps more than anyone else, have seen evidence of what depravity and evil these vile beats are capable."

"But how am I going to explain the bodies to my superiors?" wailed Lestrade. "Who in their right mind is going to accept the presence of dead, possibly headless, bodies each with a wooden stake through its heart as anything but the work of certifiable lunatics?"

"There will be no bodies," remarked Holmes tersely. "As I said before, any remains will be burnt until not a fragment of their foul presence ever existed". He pulled the van to a stop and turned to Lestrade. "I am certain that your colleagues sitting behind fully realise that the actions I am insisting on are absolutely necessary; otherwise, I do not believe they would have so willingly accompanied us today. Whatever acts we are able to accomplish during the next few hours must, perforce, remain a close secret between us all. Upon the successful completion of the tasks that lay ahead, the entire matter must be buried within our most secret thoughts forever. Am I clearly understood?" Lestrade nodded glumly.

"Good," said Holmes, "as long as we are all agreed." With that he whipped the horses into a fair trot. "I deduce the ice house is no more than a mile away," he continued, "we shall be there within the next quarter of an hour."

My friend's deductions were, as always, correct and, within the time he had so clearly specified, the huge grassy dome of the building hove into sight.

For those unfamiliar with the name, an ice house is a building in which perishable food is stored. Quite simply, a large hole is dug into the ground and a roof is added. The entire structure is then clad with brickwork and steps are then built, allowing ingress to the lower areas. Being below ground, the normal temperature is basically of a constant degree and, thus, blocks of ice are added to reduce the temperature to permit the storage of food for longer periods than would be possible in a normal pantry.

The ice house at Bascott Hall was of no exception to that normally found in the grounds of large country houses, although it was plain to see that shrubs and small trees had been planted on the roof to disguise the, somewhat, unsightly appearance of the mound containing the roof. A gate and a fence of iron railings surrounded the structure, to deter any pilfering by the local populace.

"That may cause us a little problem," mused Holmes surveying the fence. "I fear I had not allowed for this in my earlier preparations."

Holmes had drawn up the police van, slightly off the small road and the front of the building was no more than a few yards from the vehicle, and we all alighted and stood for a few moments, gazing at the iron obstacle which appeared to bar our path. It was one of the plainclothes policemen who solved the dilemma.

"Begging your pardon, Mr. Holmes. But we have a length of strong rope in the back of the van. We keep it for use in tall buildings. If we tied one end to those railings and the other to the horse, it would probably be able to pull that fence down."

Holmes turned and veritably beamed at the man who had spoken. "What a most intelligent police officer you are my good man," he cried and there was no sarcasm in the tone. "We shall do exactly as you suggest. Please be good enough to fetch the rope."

A strong horse and nine men made short shrift of the railings and several minutes following the police officer's suggestion, the remains of the fence lay in twisted confusion on the surrounding grass. Holmes walked over and studied the wooden entrance door. He beckoned me over. "See Watson, the lock has been recently used."

"How may you know that?" I enquired, "It's just a lock to me."

Holmes shook his head and raised his eyes heavenward in mild disbelief.

"Really Watson, have I taught you so little? See for yourself. The lock has been well oiled to permit ease in opening, and the person or creature who last used the facility has left certain fresh, telltale, oily finger marks on the surrounding timber." He studied the door closely and then stood back. "I estimate that those marks were made no more than a day or so ago. Possibly by the doctor. If I am correct, our quarry lies by yards hence." Holmes pulled out his Hunter and regarded the time-piece. "It is now practically a quarter to eleven o'clock," he began. "Darkness will fall at approximately nine o'clock this evening. That allows us just over ten hours in which to accomplish our terrible business. I am certain this period will be time enough, but we must proceed with haste."

Making his way back to the assembled others, he called their attention. "Gentlemen, I am now certain we have discovered the whereabouts of those vile creatures. They lay within that structure" he said, indicating the ice house. "It would seem that any security has been left to the iron fence that we have so recently demolished, for the door to the place may be stove in by a strong kick. I suggest we now avail ourselves of the items we have brought with us and gain entrance immediately. Once we are inside, and I have identified such of those devils that may rest there, I will instruct you how to proceed. Are you all ready?"

The plainclothes officers grunted their assent and Lestrade merely nodded.

"Good," said Holmes. "Then get your equipment." He turned to me. "Watson, my large carpet bag if you please".

The others moved off to the back of the police van, returning clutching stakes and the mallet. I collected the large carpet bag from the front of the vehicle and joined Holmes. "Follow me," commanded Holmes and together we approached the door to the ice house. Holmes turned to a burly policeman and indicated towards the wooden door. "Kick it in!"

The door gave after the second blow and sagged loosely against the jamb. Our party moved quickly into the dismal gloom of the interior.

"Torches ..... quickly," grunted Holmes. There followed a rustling, the sound of a match being struck and the sudden brilliance of the ignited flare. When the first torch was fully alight, the others obtained ignition from the former and slowly the cavernous confines of the ice house appeared before our peering eyes. "Follow me down the steps," said Holmes. "Be careful, all of you. There is no containing rail to prevent you failing into the pit below."

Gingerly we made our way down the stone steps. The cavern appeared to be of a depth of some thirty feet and, finally, we all stood at the base of the stair. I looked about the place. The walls of the building were circular, the roof being supported by several large pillars. The floor was of brick and appeared devoid of any item from where I stood.

"Over there," said Holmes, "beyond those pillars." We stared into the flickering gloom. Holmes seized a flaming torch from a plainclothes officer and moved quickly over to the nearest pillar. He stopped suddenly, held aloft his flaming brand and pointed.

"There, do you see," he hissed. We all looked in the direction he had indicated, and, in the spluttering illumination of his torch, five trestles were visible. Each bier bore a coffin. "Got them!" snarled Holmes, making his way to the nearest and peering into it. "Come here," he instructed the rest of us, and we made our way to stand beside him. We stared down at the contents of the box.

Before us lay the form of a beautiful girl. She was as if asleep. Her eyes were not entirely closed, and, in the light of the gathered torches, lights of pure violet sparkled from beneath her heavy lids. Her soft lips, spoilt only by tiny rivulets of carmine that oozed from each corner. "Magda" breathed Holmes. "It is surely she." He turned to the closest police officer clutching a stake and mallet. "Hand me those," he commanded.

"What are you going to do to her?" said the policeman. "Don't hurt her. She's beautiful."

Holmes said nothing. Seizing the stake and mallet, he quickly placed the point under the girl's left breast and, with one mighty blow, drove the spike deep into the chest. Bright, hot blood geysered up from within the terrible wound and fell wetly onto the brick floor. The girl's eyes flew fully open. Her formerly perfect lips grimaced in a ghastly snarl, from which uttered a terrifying screech of pure hatred and anguish, while her hands clawed ineffectually at the protruding stake. All but Holmes started back in pure horror. Holmes whirled around on us.

"Stay and look!" he screamed and, against our better feelings we returned to that awful scene. "See the teeth," said he.

We looked, and our horrified eyes clearly saw the twin, perfectly pointed, protruding incisors within the girl's mouth. The gushing blood was now a trickle and the hands which previously had clawed at the stake, sank into rest at her sides. Slowly the vicious teeth shrank back into the girl's gums and the mouth into the semblance of a slight smile. Holmes looked up at us. "She is at peace now gentlemen. Now for the others."

Quickly we searched the other coffins. Everyone contained a body. All the occupants were young girls who appeared in life to have been somewhere between the ages of eighteen and twenty-five. Of men, there were none. One by one, we collectively dispatched the remaining vampires until finally the job was done.

"The mystery of the disappearing village girls remains a mystery no longer," I began, then stopped short. Holmes had upon his face a look of pure wretchedness.

"Eldon is not here," he muttered. "All we have succeeded in accomplishing is the destruction of the host. The fountainhead of this evil plague still exists. As long as this situation remains, we are all in the most-deadly peril." He paused for a moment.

"I must think," he whispered to himself. He pulled himself together. "Bring the bodies up into the daylight," he ordered. "The coffins too. They will provide the kindling for the pyre we must now construct for the total cremation of their earthly forms. Upon no account," continued Holmes sternly, "must you remove those stakes which now impale the creatures. Do you fully understand that?" The others muttered their assent.

Within half an hour the pyre had been constructed and the corpses placed upon it. "I fear it now remains to me to undertake one final act," said Holmes gravely. "That of the decapitation of these creatures." He turned to Lestrade. "You will possibly find this act far more repugnant than the actions we have already committed, yet I assure you it is most necessary. Look away if you wish."

Lestrade waved a hand weakly, but turned his face away from the corpses. Holmes was quick. In all my experience as a doctor, I have rarely seen amputations carried out with such speed and dexterity.

The site occupied by the ice house was an obviously little tended corner of the estate, since copious amounts of dry timer were abundant. The ground atop the mound had done little to encourage the growth of the grass, which evidenced a state of near hay, and an excellent stimulant to the hungry flames which, after a short time, roared with an atavistic consistency, eagerly consuming the bodies so that, finally, nothing of them remained.

Holmes had taken no part in the cremation, merely standing apart in deep thought. As the great fire subsided, he came over to us. His eyes gleaming. "It's the only place he can be" he stated.

"I'm sorry Holmes, I cannot follow you," I said rather lamely.

"Eldon!" and he spat out the word. "He has to be back at the Hall."

"How may that be?" I enquired. "The doctor is dead. As far as we know, that creature was his sole means of conveyance. You say the Hall?" Holmes nodded tensely.

"The doctor may be dead," he began, "yet I had not taken others into account."

"Others?"

He nodded again.

"We forget that last night he added two more to his hellish brood. The policemen at the church."

"You believe they are involved?"

"I am certain of it," said Holmes. "They knew of our intention to seek out and apprehend what they will now realise is Sir Eldon, and will surely have confessed this information on their becoming part of his vile coven. I should have realised that last night."

"We must go immediately to the Hall," said I.

Holmes took out his watch and grimaced. "It is now three o'clock," he muttered. "We have five hours before darkness within which time to discover the whereabouts of that odious place and, further, put an end to that foul creation." He replaced his timepiece and shouted to Lestrade and the others. "Come on, back to the van. Be quick I say. Your very lives and eternal salvation depend upon it."

Chapter Ten

There appeared little evidence of any track or pathway leading from the ice house and, as the entire estate comprised some 350 acres of parkland, most of it wooded, Holmes decided to use the road we had travelled on earlier. We had gone about a mile when fate dealt a cruel blow.

I have made previous mention as to the poor condition of the roads within the part of the county in which we found ourselves. Holmes constantly pulled and threw the long traces here and there, directing the horses first this way and then that, yet our luck was not to last. With a tremendous jolt that nearly tossed the occupants of the front seat out onto the road, the left front wheel of the vehicle dropped into a deep rut and an ominous crack rent the quiet, summer air.

With a curse, Holmes leapt from the driving seat and knelt to inspect the damage, whilst Lestrade and I dismounted and joined the other policemen who were tumbling out from the rear of the van.

Holmes stood up. His face was stern and betrayed a degree of anxiety. "Front axle is smashed," he said curtly. "The damage is irreparable unless any one of us is a wheelwright.

"What do you propose we do now Mr. Holmes?" enquired Lestrade.

Holmes shook his head. "We will have to walk," he grunted.

"But how far is the Hall, Holmes?" said I.

"A good three miles," replied my colleague.
"But that will take us over an hour, perhaps two, if we intend to walk with the equipment we require" I continued. "Do we have enough time?"

Again, Holmes consulted his watch. "We still have over four hours of daylight remaining. Should we reach the Hall within the next two hours, there will certainly remain sufficient time for us to complete our task. But there must be no further delay."

The necessary items were quickly brought out from the back of the van and divided amongst the nine of us. Holmes insisted on carrying the large carpet bag which he held in his right hand. His other clasped the silver topped swordstick from which he was never parted. Having personally checked the items of each of the others, Holmes waved his swordstick to the highway ahead and we all marched off with a brisk step.

We made better time than I had expected, and it was, therefore, somewhat within the two hours that we reached the main gates to the Hall. They were closed, and the black ironwork shone forbiddingly in the afternoon sunlight. Holmes strode up to the gates, pushed hard and they opened. He turned and addressed us. "Looks as if we are expected" he murmured. "It will do them little good. We have over two hours in which to rid the world of this vermin. That will be sufficient for our purposes. Come gentlemen. Let us not delay."

Our party moved quickly down the long drive to the Hall. I could not help but shiver as I regarded the large windows which glared malevolently from the building. It was as if they were alive and daring us to approach the evil they contained.

On reaching the Hall we discovered the huge front door to be open. Once again, unease resurrected itself within my brain. It was all too easy. Surely the creature we believed to rest inside was aware of the possibility of our arrival. Yet, unlike the previous occasion, no one had attempted to bar our way. Something was terribly wrong. Holmes suddenly halted abruptly, looked back and studied the sky.

"Damned funny!" he ejaculated, "my shadow on the door appears to be losing its depth and texture." Suddenly his eyes widened and, when he spoke again, it was almost a snarl. "Curses! I had forgot. How stupid of me."

"What's the matter Holmes?" said I, suddenly nervous at my colleague's reactions.

"Today, now. At this very moment" hissed Holmes. "Did you not notice the sun?"

"What about it?" interrupted Lestrade.

"An eclipse," expostulated Holmes, his voice near a scream. "The sun is about to suffer an eclipse by the moon".

"Steady on Holmes" I began. "How may this have any bearing on what we have to accomplish?"

Holmes looked at me and his eyes blazed. "Don't you realise, Watson," and he spat out the words vehemently, "with the sun obscured, those monsters inside will regain their ghastly powers. If that happens we are lost."

The plainclothes officers looked uneasy at his words. "Don't you worry yourself Mr. Holmes," cried a rather burly fellow. "I reckon my mates and I are more than a match for anything inside."

Holmes turned upon the other. "Don't you yet realise," he bellowed, "any of those vile abominations that may rest within will, should they attain their full powers, be individually more than a match for the lot of us?"

The other went silent. Holmes regained his former composure.

"There is nothing for it but to proceed," he stated. "If we are quick, we may catch the monsters before they have regained their evil powers. Follow me to the cellar!"

We raced down the stone steps to the gloomy, dank basement. The failing light that seeped from the two tiny windows set high in the walls afforded sufficient illumination for us to see that the formerly unburdened trestles now supported two coffins. "At last," breathed Holmes, "we have them. Quick gentlemen, we have not a moment to lose."

The first coffin contained the body of one of the policemen. He lay still, dressed in his police uniform, to all intents asleep. As we gazed on his supine form, his eyes flew open and focussed upon the assembled group. Slowly his mouth drew back forming a dreadful smirk which revealed those terrible incisors. He hissed vehemently and attempted to rise from his coffin. Holmes was too quick. In what seemed one movement, he thrust a stake into the creature's chest and, with a single blow, drove the sharp point deep into the body. The odious form arched in agony and, from the lips, came forth a scream of pure frustrated anger. Blood spurted in hot gusts from the dreadful wound as the body slowly sank back into the coffin.

"Quick!" shouted Holmes. "Now the other."

We raced to the next coffin, but it was empty. For a second we all stood transfixed at the sight of the vacant box.

"Good God," breathed Holmes. "The creature is at large."

Our deliberations were suddenly interrupted by a dreadful cry. We spun about. One of the plainclothes policemen in our party, writhed vainly within the grip of the second uniformed officer. The beast which had hold of the unfortunate man, hissed and snarled horribly as it attempted to sink its fangs into the other's neck.

We were all dumbfounded with fear and loathing. Holmes was the first to recover. With two strides he was beside the struggling bodies. His right arm flew up and the contents of a bottle of holy water drenched the pair. The effect was instantaneous. The creature screamed in agony and released the plainclothes officer who fell to the floor. Where the holy water had touched the other, the flesh suppurated, boiled and fell away. Slowly the vile body sank to the floor of the cellar and, before our astonished eyes, swirls of thin smoke began to rise from within the soiled uniform.

"Give me a stake and a mallet," commanded Holmes. I handed him mine. Holmes quickly knelt beside the decomposing carcass and drove the stake into the other's body. Fumbling briefly within his top coat, Holmes extricated the butcher's cleaver and, with a single stroke, severed what remained of the rotting neck. He stood up, panting from is exertions.
"That's the lot of them, then," said Lestrade.

Holmes shook his head. "I fear not," he muttered. "All we have accomplished is to destroy what I believe are the brood. The master remains at large. If we fail to discover and destroy that foul incarnation, our efforts will have been in vain."

As if in answer to his statement, a hollow most evil chuckle, which was more a bloated gurgle, resounded throughout the dark confines of the cellar. We spun round as one. Standing beside a third coffin which, in the gloom, we had failed to notice, stood a figure. The form was of a man, slightly above medium height. The figure appeared to be surrounded by a mauve aura which shimmered malevolently in the gloom and highlighted the awful face. The eyes were distended and glowed red with an unholy gleam. The pupils of the blackest coal, held us all in a deadly unhallowed glare. The face was swollen and suffused with a ghastly pallor. The large, drooling lips drawn back from that awful maw, betrayed broken, slime coated teeth from which the incisors protruded sharply above a bloated, serpentine tongue which flicked venomously within the monstrous head.

The creature spoke at last. "Holmes? It is Holmes, is it not?"

"It is I," hissed my colleague. "And you are Sir Eldon Manning."

The face of the other grinned evilly. "You appear to have ruined such as I have created here," he said, and his words oozed with the sickly treacle of depraved evil. "No matter, I shall begin anew."

"That you shall never do," replied Holmes, his voice steady and controlled. "Your vile, repugnant time upon this world is ended."

Once again, the cellar reverberated with that ghastly chuckle. "I fear you have misjudged my powers, Holmes," said the creature. "Darkness allows me unlimited abilities over which even you and your colleagues will be as weaklings. Let me demonstrate a small exercise for you."

The creature turned its awful gaze upon the empty bottle of holy water which Holmes still held in his hand. For a moment nothing happened. Then the flask began to glow. Holmes let out an oath and dropped the bottle.

The creature laughed harshly. "You have misjudged me Holmes," it croaked. "Such impedimenta are of little value against one who is of such exalted order among followers of the left-hand path. Whereas others, who are not so highly placed, have cause to fear that water you so highly prize. It is, to me, about as injurious as a cup of cold coffee."

Holmes drew back apace. "You may not avoid the stake," he said quietly. "Even for you, it will mean your complete destruction."

The apparition smiled horribly. "In that respect you are correct," said the creature. "However," it continued, "to effect that action requires strength."

With those words, Sir Eldon turned his gaze upon us. His eyes appeared to grow large within that terrible face. Suddenly I felt my body devoid of any action and my will recede. I was as a rabbit within the stare of a snake. I could move my eyes and noticed the others appeared to be in a similar trance. Only Holmes evidenced any degree of control and he, I saw, fought grimly against the awful power which had ensnared the others.

Sir Eldon came slowly towards us. His hideous face gleamed with a dreadful varnish of unholy victory. We were at the fiend's mercy. At that precise moment, Holmes overcame his mental struggle. In an action too quick for the normal eye, he drew out his sword from its cane and plunged the entire length of steel into the creature's chest. Sir Eldon shrieked and staggered back. Immediately, the somnambulant force, which had previously possessed me, disappeared.

I heard Holmes shout. "Quick Watson, a stake!"

Galvanised into action by my friend's order, I looked about. One stake rested on the floor of the cellar by Lestrade's feet. I picked it up and turned to Holmes.

"Into the heart!" cried Holmes. "I have no mallet."

"Use the wound from the sword," cried Holmes. "For God's sake be quick!"

Sir Eldon sprawled against a wall of the cellar. Those dreadful eyes now lustreless. I went over – then stopped.

"What's the matter?" shouted Holmes.

I hesitated still. My Hippocratic Oath screamed salvation not murder, to the injured creature slouching before me. "But he's alive," I cried.

Holmes acted swiftly. Seizing the stake from my hand he drove the timber deep into the sword's wound. Sir Eldon Manning collapsed upon the ground. Holmes turned to me. "Why did you desist?"

"I forgot the nature of the beast for a moment," I replied lamely. "Only seeing before me an injured fellow human being. My training as a doctor compelled me to withhold any act which would cause further harm. I'm sorry, Holmes."

"Never mind old friend," said Holmes patting me on the shoulder. "All has been done that should be done. Let us see to our colleagues."

On regaining the presence of the others, "The vampire is able to exert a wave of intense hypnotic power," explained Holmes. "It is how he is able to restrain an otherwise unwilling victim. As soon as I broke that spell by my sword thrust, the creature's own will was destroyed and your own returned to you."

"Well I never," began Lestrade, then stopped abruptly, pointing beyond Holmes's back. "My God," he cried, "look!"

We all looked. Sir Eldon Manning was climbing to his feet. The stake was still protruding from within his body, caked in blood that dripped slowly from the unimpeded end. The devilish glare had returned to those dreadful eyes, and his mouth grinned horribly.

"You have failed Holmes," said a mouth filled with a detritus of bright blood. The fiend thumped its chest some two to three inches from where the stake protruded. "You missed the heart, and I am not destroyed. Now I shall leave you, but rest assured I shall be back and, next time, you will all be mine for eternity." With that, the odious creature leapt for the cellar steps, mounted them nimbly, threw shut the heavy door and disappeared.

"After him!" cried Holmes and, together we scrambled to the steps and up to the door which, unlocked, gave upon a push. We stood panting in the large hallway.

"To the entrance," cried Holmes. "The creature must have left the building." Holmes and I were first to the door and out onto the paving stones.

"Look," cried Holmes, "there it is".

I looked in the direction to which he pointed and saw a figure running across the parkland in the direction of a thick cluster of trees. Suddenly the pace of the fiend altered and became sluggish. Then the figure stopped completely and raised its arms to the sky.

"Whatever is wrong with the vile thing?" I enquired.

Holmes folded his arms across his chest and smiled softly. "We have been saved by a miracle," he said quietly. "An astronomical miracle, although I like to believe it to be the work of a higher authority." He turned to me and finding me somewhat perplexed continued. "The eclipse is passing. The full effect of the sun's rays is upon the cursed demon, against which he has no defence."

We both stared out over the park at the figure of Sir Eldon Manning. For a few seconds the figure writhed grotesquely within the brightening sunlight. It then suddenly appeared to explode into a myriad of tiny atoms which caught the slight breeze and dispersed completely, until nothing remained.

"That is the end of it" remarked Holmes sagely.

Chapter Eleven

It was some three days later, as we sat together in Baker Street, taking afternoon tea that Mrs. Hudson ushered Inspector Lestrade into our rooms. Our recent actions, we were informed, enjoyed, and would forever enjoy, the secrecy on which we had all previously agreed in Dedham.

Both the vicar's and the doctor's deaths were being put down to unavoidable accidents; the former through lack of care in placing the heavy cross in a situation where it may, and did, fall upon him; and the latter, through the incautious driving of his carriage.

Local constabulary continued their fruitless search for the ferocious animal which had so cruelly slain the police officers while the fire at the ice house had been put down to mischievous lads.

The remains of the bonfire to the front of Bascott Hall and the rather oily stain in the parkland remained a mystery, as did the disappearance of Sir Eldon Manning but, as the latter barely had occasion to meet and speak with anyone in the locality, the conundrum was expected to last but a few weeks -- if that.

Holmes was ever the generous, respectful host. "Perhaps I may offer you a glass of the finest Madeira?" he enquired. Lestrade eagerly accepted the proffered drink, sat down where Holmes indicated yet, for a few moments, took no sip of the liquid.

Holmes noticed. "Your visit to us today was not just to appraise Watson and me of the situation following our visit to Dedham I surmise, Inspector," he said. "From your apparent lack of interest in consuming one of the finest wines in my cellar, I deduce you have a problem which you may wish to impart."

For a few seconds Lestrade studied the liquid contents of his glass, and then he spoke. "A situation has arisen in Whitechapel," he began. "Sir Charles Warren, himself, has asked me to look into the matter. Holmes chuckled briefly at the mention of the other's name, yet I could see, by the gleam in his eye, that he was interested.

"If the matter has become the concern of such an exalted individual as the Commissioner of Police," he began, "it can be no minor situation, more easily dealt with by the local constabulary. Pray, tell me more."

Lestrade finally took a large sip from his glass, swallowed the contents a little too quickly, and looked up at Holmes.

"During the past few weeks, two women – both known prostitutes – have been done to death in the East End of the capital," he said slowly.

Holmes pursed his lips. "Murder and mayhem haunt those dingy streets and dark alleyways with the regularity of a winter fog he remarked. "Why does the death of two more provoke the attention of Sir Charles?"

"It is the method of their death" replied Lestrade. "Each woman had her throat cut, and both were practically disembowelled. Sir Charles fears we may be looking for a maniac. If that thought becomes common knowledge, it could create an outraged mob and set alight the whole east end."

"I see," said Holmes sagely. "And do you have any indication as to who or what may be responsible for these outrages?"

Lestrade nodded. "We have received a note on a piece of paper. The writing appears to be in human blood and signed by an individual purporting to be the killer."

Holmes slapped his thigh. "Then if you have the murderer's name, surely you have little else to do but to arrest the individual," he ejaculated. "What can be easier than that?

Lestrade shook his head. "It's not that simple," he began.

Holmes interrupted impatiently. "For God's sake man, why do you tarry?"

"We haven't a name as such," said Lestrade lamely. "More of a nickname. That's why we cannot arrest the person."

Holmes sank back in his chair and folded his hands over his chest. "Very well, what does this killer call himself?"

Lestrade took a piece of rumpled paper out of his waistcoat pocket -- it was little more than a scrap -- and handed it to Holmes. My colleague studied the item, then pursed his lips, raised an eyebrow and murmured softly.

"Jack the Ripper."

- End -

Also from MX Publishing

MX Publishing is the world's largest specialist Sherlock Holmes publisher, with over a hundred titles and fifty authors creating the latest in Sherlock Holmes fiction and non-fiction.

From traditional short stories and novels to travel guides and quiz books, MX Publishing cater for all Holmes fans.

The collection includes leading titles such as *Benedict Cumberbatch In Transition* and *The Norwood Author* which won the 2011 Howlett Award (Sherlock Holmes Book of the Year).

MX Publishing also has one of the largest communities of Holmes fans on Facebook with regular contributions from dozens of authors.

www.mxpublishing.com

Also from MX Publishing

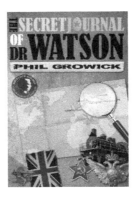

"Phil Growick's, "The Secret Journal of Dr. Watson", is an adventure which takes place in the latter part of Holmes and Watson's lives. They are entrusted by HM Government (although not officially) and the King no less to undertake a rescue mission to save the Romanovs, Russia's Royal family from a grisly end at the hand of the Bolsheviks. There is a wealth of detail in the story but not so much as would detract us from the enjoyment of the story. Espionage, counter-espionage, the ace of spies himself, double-agents, double-crossers...all these flit across the pages in a realistic and exciting way. All the characters are extremely well-drawn and Mr. Growick, most importantly, does not falter with a very good ear for Holmesian dialogue indeed. Highly recommended. A five-star effort."
The Baker Street Society

www.mxpublishing.com

Also from MX Publishing

The Missing Authors Series

Sherlock Holmes and The Adventure of The Grinning Cat
Sherlock Holmes and The Nautilus Adventure
Sherlock Holmes and The Round Table Adventure

"Joseph Svec, III is brilliant in entwining two endearing and enduring classics of literature, blending the factual with the fantastical; the playful with the pensive; and the mischievous with the mysterious. We shall, all of us young and old, benefit with a cup of tea, a tranquil afternoon, and a copy of Sherlock Holmes, The Adventure of the Grinning Cat."

Amador County Holmes Hounds Sherlockian Society

www.mxpublishing.com

Also from MX Publishing

The Detective and The Woman Series

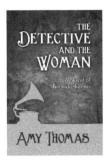 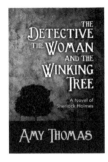 

The Detective and The Woman
The Detective, The Woman and The Winking Tree
The Detective, The Woman and The Silent Hive

"The book is entertaining, puzzling and a lot of fun. I believe the author has hit on the only type of long-term relationship possible for Sherlock Holmes and Irene Adler. The details of the narrative only add force to the romantic defects we expect in both of them and their growth and development are truly marvelous to watch. This is not a love story. Instead, it is a coming-of-age tale starring two of our favorite characters."
Philip K Jones

Also from MX Publishing

The Sherlock Holmes and Enoch Hale Series

 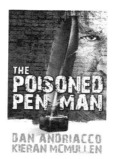 

The Amateur Executioner
The Poisoned Penman
The Egyptian Curse

"The Amateur Executioner: Enoch Hale Meets Sherlock Holmes", the first collaboration between Dan Andriacco and Kieran McMullen, concerns the possibility of a Fenian attack in London. Hale, a native Bostonian, is a reporter for London's Central News Syndicate - where, in 1920, Horace Harker is still a familiar figure, though far from revered. "The Amateur Executioner" takes us into an ambiguous and murky world where right and wrong aren't always distinguishable. I look forward to reading more about Enoch Hale."
Sherlock Holmes Society of London

www.mxpublishing.com

Also from MX Publishing

Sherlock Holmes novellas in verse

  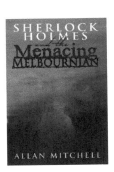

All four novellas have been released also in audio format with narration by Steve White

Sherlock Holmes and The Menacing Moors
Sherlock Holmes and The Menacing Metropolis
Sherlock Holmes and The Menacing Melbournian
Sherlock Holmes and The Menacing Monk

"The story is really good and the Herculean effort it must have been to write it all in verse—well, my hat is off to you, Mr. Allan Mitchell! I wouldn't dream of seeing such work get less than five plus stars from me..." **The Raven**

Also from MX Publishing

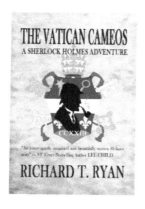

When the papal apartments are burgled in 1901, Sherlock Holmes is summoned to Rome by Pope Leo XII. After learning from the pontiff that several priceless cameos that could prove compromising to the church, and perhaps determine the future of the newly unified Italy, have been stolen, Holmes is asked to recover them. In a parallel story, Michelangelo, the toast of Rome in 1501 after the unveiling of his Pieta, is commissioned by Pope Alexander VI, the last of the Borgia pontiffs, with creating the cameos that will bedevil Holmes and the papacy four centuries later. For fans of Conan Doyle's immortal detective, the game is always afoot. However, the great detective has never encountered an adversary quite like the one with whom he crosses swords in "The Vatican Cameos."

"An extravagantly imagined and beautifully written Holmes story"
(Lee Child, NY Times Bestselling author, Jack Reacher series)

Lightning Source UK Ltd.
Milton Keynes UK
UKHW02f0640051217
313899UK00010B/908/P